THIS ONE IS FOR MY
THREE DAUGHTERS,
EVA,
ELLA,
AND
CLAIRE:
ALWAYS MY ANGELS.

SOME KIND OF COURAGE

DAN GEMEINHART

SCHOLASTIC INC.

Copyright © 2016 by Dan Gemeinhart

This book was originally published in hardcover by Scholastic Press in 2016.

All rights reserved. Published by Scholastic Inc., *Publishers since 1920.* SCHOLASTIC and associated logos are trademarks and/or registered trademarks of Scholastic Inc.

The publisher does not have any control over and does not assume any responsibility for author or third-party websites or their content.

ISBN 978-0-545-66582-7

10 9 8 7   18 19 20 21

Printed in the U.S.A. 40
First printing 2017

Book design by Nina Goffi

CHAPTER
I

OCTOBER. 1890
OLD MISSION, WASHINGTON

I reckoned it was the coldest, darkest hour of the night. That still hour just before dawn. Mama always called it the "angels and devils hour," on account of how only angels or demons would have any work worth doing at a time like that. I didn't know if I was doing the Lord's work or the Devil's, but I knew that it had to be done and the time had sure enough come to do it.

I'd been lying too many sleepless hours in my sorry straw-stuffed bed, waiting for the old man to finally fall dead asleep. My plan had been burning all night in my mind like the last glowing embers in the fireplace, keeping my heart awake. Truth be told, my hands were a bit shaky as I finally crept, as quiet as could be, across the cabin's dirt floor toward where he lay snoring. And it weren't just the cold making 'em shake, neither. But my heart was as steady as a true horse, heading toward home.

My leather bag was already thrown over my shoulder. I'd slipped it on without him seeing, before I'd curled up under my blanket. And my boots were still on my feet. He'd been too drunk to notice me not taking 'em off.

All I needed was the money. And the gun. And then to hit the trail running.

The money was piled on a shelf up on the wall by his bed. I licked my lips and crept closer, my feet finding a path in the barely lit darkness. I could see the barrel of the pistol, gleaming in the dim red light of the coals, on the crate beneath the shelf. It was right within reach of the arm the old man had thrown across his face.

Barely breathing, I took the last few steps and reached up with my left hand. My fingers closed around the crumpled stack of dirty greenbacks, and with a smooth and silent motion I slipped them off the shelf. *It ain't stealing*, I told myself. *This money belongs to me, by all rights.* I ain't sure I convinced myself, and doubt chewed on my insides. But there weren't no choice.

I crouched and turned toward the pistol, but as I did my foot kicked an empty booze bottle. It spun in the shadows and rattled against another one with a loud *clink* that shattered the quiet of the cabin.

The old man's snoring stopped in mid-breath with a snort. His arm jerked up from his face, and two red eyes glared at me, confused but already angry. They narrowed when they saw the money clutched in my hand, and his top lip pulled back in a snarl.

"What're you doing, boy?" he asked in his high, piercing whine of a voice. Lord, how I had learned to hate that voice of his.

I froze, too scared to answer.

He blinked, his drunken brain no doubt starting to make sense of what was happening. He started to sit up, then stopped. We both looked at the gun at the same time. There was one tight, breathless moment when we both knew what we were gonna do.

Our bodies lunged and our hands struck like snakes. He was closer, but I was quicker, and when I stumbled back two steps the gun was gripped tight in my right hand.

It was his turn to freeze, and he did.

"What're you doing, boy?" he asked again, but now his voice had a sure enough nervous tremble in it.

"You had no right to sell her," I said. I was ashamed of how my voice quivered, not at all like a man's. Not at all like my papa's.

The old man grimaced like he'd just taken a suck on a fresh lemon.

" 'Course I did, boy. She was *mine*. And I need the money to pay for all the food you eat."

My underfed belly rumbled the truth to his lie, and I shook my head.

"No, sir. I work for my keep, and I work hard. And that horse was mine. You got this money by selling my horse, so it's my money. And I'm gonna use it to get her back." *And you wouldn't be using this money for food, neither, but for more bottles of Dutch John's brandy*, I wanted to say. But my mama had taught me better manners than that, and I held my tongue.

He slid his feet out of bed and sat up. I took another step back.

"Give me my money and git back in bed," he said. "You ain't never gonna shoot me."

He started to stand up but stopped when I cocked the hammer of the gun back with a *click* that rang clear as a church bell on Sunday.

"I will," I said. "I sure enough will, Mr. Grissom. I ain't never shot a man, sir, and I hope I never do. But I'm gonna get my horse back. And if you try to stop me, I swear I will put a bullet in you." My voice still had that scared-boy shake in it, but underneath the shake was a hardness that I know we both heard. An iron hardness that sounded an awful lot like the truth.

His eyes squinted uncertainly at me.

"Your pa left you in my care, boy, along with your horse and—"

"My papa didn't have a choice. And I know he'd want me to go after her, no matter what." I swallowed and hoped it was true. It was so hard to know.

"But that's my gun! You can't take my gun!" The high whine came back into his voice.

I shook my head again.

"No, sir. This was my papa's gun. He taught me to shoot with it. He—" My voice caught in my throat, and I had to stop to swallow down the sadness that was always there, ready to rise up and choke me. "He'd want it to be mine. If something needs shooting, you've still got your rifle."

I stuffed the money into my bag and backed up to the plank door. I opened it with my free hand, the gun still raised between us.

"You can't take all that money, boy! It's all I've got! I'll starve!"

I knew it wasn't true, but I paused there in that doorway. It's sure enough hard sometimes to tell right from wrong. He'd gotten the money from selling my horse, and I knew I'd need it to buy her back. And I knew the money was more likely to go to liquor than biscuits. But I could feel my mama's eyes on me, watching. And my papa's. I wanted to do 'em proud, but right and wrong were lost in the dark of the cabin. I clenched my teeth. *A man's only as good as he treats his enemies*, Papa had said.

My hand slid back into my bag and found the eight ten-dollar bills. I pulled one out and set it on the handle of the ax leaning by the door.

"There you go, sir. I'll be going now. You won't be seeing me again."

I was mostly out the door when he whined his parting words.

"He's long gone, you know! He's at least twelve hours ahead, with you on foot and him riding. You'll never catch him, boy."

My teeth ground hard against each other. I lowered the gun and looked him straight in his stubbly face.

"I will, sir," I said. "I will get her back."

I let the door close behind me and without a look back I walked off as quick as I could through the darkness. The sky beyond the hills was just beginning to grow pale with the coming day. The angels and the devils could all go to sleep now. But I sure enough hoped that one angel would stay up and keep by my side.

The grass and the stones and the dirt ruts of the road were covered in an icy white blanket of morning frost, and my boots crunched with each step.

I'm coming for you, sweet Sarah girl, I thought to myself. I would find her, and I would get her back. I knew I would. Or I'd sure enough die trying.

CHAPTER
2

I made good time downriver, my feet eating up miles as fast as my legs would move 'em. By the time the whole round sun sat in the sky I was already halfway to Wenatchee, where I hoped to catch the man who had my horse.

The leaves on the trees by the river were already into their fall changing, painting my path with all their reds and yellows and oranges. Funny how them colors are thought to be such a beautiful thing, when what it really amounts to is their dying. It was pretty, though, anyway. Puffy pink sunrise clouds hung in the sky above the foothills of the mountains that crowded all around me and the river. It was the kind of sight that would have made Mama put her hand to her cheek and say, *"Oh, bless the world for its beauty!"* I did raise my head to take it in from time to time, for her sake. But I kept my hand on the bulge of the gun in my satchel. The world sure enough ain't *all* beauty.

I was still trying to get my head around how Mr. Grissom had sold my Sarah away from me. I should have known. I kicked myself for not seeing it, for not getting suspicious at the way he and the stranger, Mr. Ezra Bishop, had been talking. How they'd whisper and hush when I came around. It had been strange, but I reckoned I knew better than to question or bother Mr. Grissom. And then he'd sent me off, on that fool's errand to check his stock pens up on the ridge. By the time I'd gotten back, Ezra Bishop and his string of ponies were gone and night was coming on. I'd done my normal chores and duties and it wasn't 'til after dinner, when

Mr. Grissom was halfway into his first bottle, that I'd gone out to feed and brush Sarah and found her stall empty.

My heart burned with a fierce kind of anger. I kicked at the rocks in the ruts, spitting mad just thinking about it. My sweet girl Sarah. She was all I had left in the world. I shook my head and cut away from the road, through the brush down to the river.

The Wenatchee River was calm here, flowing smooth and quiet down to the mighty Columbia. I knelt on the smooth round stones of her bank and scooped the water up to my mouth with both hands. My ears filled with the gentle, near and far sound of the water as it bubbled 'round rocks and tumbled its way over little dips. *"That's the voice of the river,"* I could hear Mama's voice say. *"A river tells a different story to every living soul. It's got one just for you, Joseph, if you listen."* I couldn't help but wonder what kinda story the river was telling me now, as I was heading alone down this road with a gun in my satchel and a grudge in my heart. I didn't know if I would like it. Or if I'd like the ending.

I drank my fill in slurping handfuls, but the water had lost some of its sweetness. It wasn't until I stood up and turned back toward the road that I saw the great pine just in the distance, the one standing watch over the small grassy clearing dotted with crude stones and wooden crosses.

I'd darn near missed it. I'd sure enough been lost in my thoughts, thoughts of what had happened and what might be coming. I'd darn near missed it.

I looked down the road toward Wenatchee. I didn't have any time to lose, but I reckoned a few minutes more wouldn't weigh much against the hours I had to make up.

And if I really wasn't coming back, I knew there weren't no way I could leave without saying good-bye to Papa.

My anger melted away like the morning frost as I made my way over to the little graveyard. There were only a handful of graves, lovingly but clumsily marked.

I knew right where his grave was, there in the knee-high grass. I'd visited it enough times in the months since he'd died, any time I could find when Mr. Grissom would let me slip away.

It weren't even a cross, just a wooden marker cut from an old door. I'd had no real money, and no way to get anything better. I'd carved the words into the wood myself.

WILLIAM JOHNSON, it said. 1855–1890. That was it. I'd run out of room. There was too much to say, far too much, to fit on that old board. I could have had a forest of boards for carving and not had enough space to say everything that was in my heart.

"Hey, Papa," I whispered, looking down at his grave. There weren't no breeze and the grass stood still, like it were listening.

"Well, I'm off. Mr. Grissom done sold Sarah off, and I aim to get her back. I don't know that I'll ever be coming back here." I blew out a bitter breath and looked away from his leaning board. It sure enough didn't feel right, leaving him here with this sorry marker, with no family around to lay flowers or remember him. But I s'pose leaving graves behind is just something you do in this life, until you get to your own. I rubbed at my nose and sniffled.

"I won't never forget nothing you told me, Papa. I'll make you proud. I swear and I promise that I will." I took just one breath to calm the hard lump in my throat. I weren't going to say my last words to Papa like a crying little boy. I was his son, and I aimed to live up to that.

I sniffed again and nodded. "Yes, sir. There are things that have to be done in this world, and it's our duty to do 'em right. Like you always said. And I intend to do this, and do it right." I bent down and yanked up some grass that had grown too long, nearly covering his name. I saw a little stone there, round and white, resting up against his grave marker. I picked it up and slipped it into my pocket.

"Good-bye, Papa," I said, and then turned and walked away.

I knew the names of the folks in the few scattered homesteads and cabins I passed, some right on the wagon road and some farther away, tucked up by the hills. It was full morning now, and twists of smoke curled from the chimneys or pipes of most of the homes. There were some sounds here and there of chopping wood or other labor, but I didn't slow or stop. Not until Frank Jameson's place, anyway. It was right there by the road. He was out sitting on a stump, eating, and he saw me coming.

"Mornin', Joseph," he said as I walked up. He wiped his hand on his pants and held it out to me to shake. I smelled the sweet breakfast smell of his pancakes and my mouth went right to watering but I bit my tongue and shook his hand.

"Morning, Mr. Jameson."

"Mr. Grissom's got you out on the trail early today, don't he? What business he got you on?"

"It's business of my own today, sir. Me and Mr. Grissom have parted ways."

Mr. Jameson's eyebrows went up. "That right? Well, that's much more in your favor than his."

The sun was still rising higher and I felt the trail pulling me on, so I cut right to it.

"Did a man pass through here last night, sir? A Mr. Bishop, with a string of ponies?"

Mr. Jameson poked at some food in his cheek with his tongue and nodded.

"Uh-huh," he said. "Couple hours before sunset. Heading down Wenatchee way, he said. Asked if I had any horses to sell." He squinched up one eye and looked at me. "I coulda swore I saw that Indian filly of yours in there with his, Joseph. The red-and-white paint?"

I gritted my teeth and nodded.

"Yes, sir. Mr. Grissom—" I had to stop for a step to keep my anger down and my words civil. "Mr. Grissom sold her in my absence, and I aim to catch up to Mr. Bishop and buy her back."

The muscles in Mr. Jameson's jaw tightened with an angry ripple.

"Sold your horse? That old cuss sold your horse?"

"Yes, sir. But I reckon I'll find Mr. Bishop in Wenatchee and have it all straightened out by lunchtime."

"Well. Yeah. I do hope so, Joseph."

"Thank you, sir. I best be going."

I was set to leave, but a thought had been nagging me all morning, and I had to put it to rest. I reached into my satchel, pulled out my papa's pistol, and held it out to Mr. Jameson, grip-first.

"Could you please return this to Mr. Grissom, sir, next time you see him?"

"Ain't that your papa's pistol?"

"Yes, sir. Well, it was. And I felt I had the right to take it. But . . . I reckon I changed my mind. My papa said if Mr. Grissom were to take care of me, all our supplies and goods were his. I s'pose that includes his gun along with the rest."

I locked my eyes on Mr. Jameson's, trying to keep the sounds and sights of my papa's death out of my mind. They came back to me sometimes too strong, and I needed to keep myself steady. But I'd never forget that awful day. The wagon jerking and turning over, rolling down that hill, my papa crushed beneath it. The hours of sitting there watching him die, with no doctor and nothing to be done. The tears that had leaked stubbornly from his eyes, his ragged whisper over and over, *"I'm sorry, son. I'm so sorry."* Mr. Grissom had come along, heading to his measly cabin, and I s'pose he'd done his best to help. But there was no helping what was wrong with my papa, and my papa'd known it. With his last breaths he'd begged Mr. Grissom to care for me, and promised him all our homesteading goods. I shook my head to chase them clinging ghosts away.

Mr. Jameson looked angry, but I knew his anger weren't for me.

"No, son. I aim to give Mr. Grissom *something* next time I see him, but it ain't gonna be your papa's gun. That is yours, Joseph. It was your papa's, and now it's yours, true as anything. I wouldn't call what that dog did takin' care of you, neither . . . more like takin' advantage."

His eyes narrowed and his voice got lower.

"Listen, son. You may need that gun, up ahead. Mr. Bishop seemed in a hurry, and he's on horseback. You may have to chase him up and over the mountains. There's bears up there, and plenty of rattlesnakes. And you, what, twelve?"

"I'll be thirteen in February, sir. I ain't no boy."

Mr. Jameson nodded. "Maybe not. But you ain't quite a man yet, neither, and this ain't always friendly country." He pushed the gun back toward me. "You take that, and you feel good about it. Your papa would want you to."

His last words got me. I bit my lip and slid the gun back into my satchel.

"Now, you listen," Mr. Jameson continued. "You be real careful with that Ezra Bishop fella. He had an ugly way about him, and he's got a bad name 'round here. You keep your wits about you, and don't give him a red cent 'til he hands you the bridle to that pony of yours."

"Yes, sir. All right."

"Hold on a bit," he said, then disappeared into his cabin. He came back out with a handkerchief tied in a bundle. "There's two pancakes in here, and a piece of salt pork. Eat it as you walk." I opened my mouth to protest, but he held up his hand. "No use fighting. I ain't sending you off with an empty stomach."

"Thank you, sir. I sure do—"

"I know, I know. Now get going. You got a lot ahead of you."

I was only a few paces down the road when he called out, "She didn't want to leave you, you know."

"Sir?"

"Your horse. What's her name?"

"Sarah," I said, turning back.

"Right. Well, she was fighting him the whole way, jerking and pulling, trying to get back to you. Never seen a broke horse fight like that. It was everything he could do to keep her going. Madder than a hornet, he was." His last words hung with a warning behind them. Like he was trying to tell me something, but was afraid to. My hands clenched into fists.

"Was he whipping her?" I asked. "Was he whipping my horse, Mr. Jameson?" My voice was winter steel, cold and hard.

Mr. Jameson licked his lips and squinted, then nodded.

"Yes, son. His arm is gonna be clean wore off by the time he gets to Wenatchee, he was whipping her so hard to keep her moving."

My fingernails bit like rabid dogs into my palms. My breath shook through my nostrils. I didn't trust my voice to talk, or my heart to say any words my mama would've approved of. Ezra Bishop was whipping my horse? He was whipping my sweet Sarah?

I turned and marched quick and dark as thunder toward Wenatchee, glad for the gun I carried.

CHAPTER
3

Wenatchee was the biggest town around, but it weren't really much of a town at all. Miller Road was the only real street, and it was just a dusty dirt track winding through sagebrush and boulders. All the people lived at their homesteads and orchards, out amongst the brown hills and rocky canyons. The town itself was only a few buildings—a hotel, a couple of houses, a government building for filing claims and such. At the end of this little cluster of wooden buildings was my destination: the Miller-Freer Trading Post.

The trading post was never much to look at. A shabby little low building, with a couple of grimy windows and a sagging roof. I shook my head and cursed softly when I saw it, but not because it was small and plain. I cursed 'cause I knew right off that what I was after weren't there.

There were no horses tied up at the rail out front. The corral around back was empty. It was the same story at the few other buildings that made up the town of Wenatchee.

Ezra Bishop was gone, and my Sarah with him. Disappointment hit my heart like a snakebite, but my feet didn't slow. They sure enough sped up. I weren't gonna give up, and the more behind I fell, the faster I'd have to go to catch up.

I strode right up toward the door. I was so set on what I had to do, I didn't even see the body sitting silent on the ground, leaned up against the trading post's log walls in the shadows of the roof overhang. I jumped back, startled, when two legs shifted in the dust to keep me from tripping on 'em.

"Lord, I'm sorry, I—" My words cut off when I'd seen his face.

He was a Chinese. And just a boy, not any older than me and maybe a bit younger. He blinked at me, and I could tell I'd just woken him up. He pulled his legs up quick to his chest and turned his head away, like maybe he was afraid I was gonna hit him.

I'd seen Chinese before, of course. There were plenty of 'em in the country, mining and panning for gold once the railroads were mostly built. They kept to themselves, though, and I'd never seen one up close.

"It's all right," I said quickly. "I just didn't see you there, is all." His face stayed pointed away from me. He was breathing and blinking fast, and I could see the nervous swallowing in his throat. He sure enough looked scared. I looked up and down the road again, but I didn't see any sign of any more Chinese.

"Sorry," I said again, then walked past him into the trading post.

The light was dim through the dirty windows. Mr. Miller was sitting on a barrel behind a rough counter. Sacks and crates and boxes of goods were piled all about.

"Hello, sir."

Mr. Miller spit a stream of dirty brown tobacco juice into a bucket at his feet and lifted his chin at me.

"Mornin'."

"Did a man named Ezra Bishop stop in here last night or this morning?"

Mr. Miller nodded and moved the chaw around in his mouth.

"Yep."

"When did he leave?"

Mr. Miller squinted thoughtfully, then shrugged.

"Mm. Sometime last night, I s'pose. 'Round sunset. Didn't stop long. Got some coffee 'n flour. Asked around a bit about horses. Then he was gone."

"What's he want the horses for?"

Mr. Miller shrugged again, then leaned down and spit.

"Do you know where he's headed? Which way he went?"

Mr. Miller jerked his head back over his shoulder in a vaguely southward direction.

"Said somethin' 'bout Walla Walla. Took off down Rock Island way, last I saw."

"Walla Walla?" My heart dropped. Walla Walla was clear across the state. A couple hundred miles, I reckoned. My hands went all sweaty and my belly tightened. I felt like I could feel my Sarah being dragged farther and farther out of my reach. I licked my lips and shifted restless from foot to foot. "How you s'pose he's gonna get there?"

Mr. Miller had never been one for conversation and I could tell he was gettin' good and bored with our talking. He scowled and screwed his eyes up at me.

"Heck, boy, I don't know. Up and over Colockum and down through Robber's Roost, I s'pose. T'ain't no concern of mine and it probably ain't none of yours, neither. You here to buy somethin' or just to jaw at me all morning?"

"No, sir. I appreciate your help." I was backing toward the door when I remembered the boy outside. "Who's the boy out front, sir?"

Mr. Miller grimaced. "What, the Chinaman? He still there?" He shook his head and spit.

Chinaman. I heard the word in my mind, then my mama's voice. I'd said it once, the year before, after we'd passed a group of Chinese on the road to Yakima.

"*I don't like that word, Joseph,*" she'd said. "*It's an ugly word, and I don't want you saying it.*" I'd been confused. Everyone called them Chinamen. I didn't know there was another word for 'em.

"*It ain't a curse word, Mama,*" I'd argued.

She'd pursed her lips. "*Any word can be an ugly word if you say it ugly. And people say that word ugly, Joseph, nearly every time. It sounds hateful and I don't like it. They're people just like us, at the end of the day. In the Lord's eyes, if not in His people's.*"

Mama had always been my measure of goodness. And always would be. I hadn't said *Chinaman* since.

"That ain't no man," I answered Mr. Miller. "He's just a boy. Where're his people?"

"Under a few feet of dirt and rocks," he said, matter-of-factly. "Him and a couple of grown ones limped into town three days ago. The others were sick as dogs. Died 'fore sunset. Not sure of what."

I stared at him. "So he's all by himself? He ain't got no family or nothing?"

"Nope. Been sitting there like that ever since he showed up three days ago. Must be hungry as a bear."

My belly dropped down to the rough board floor.

"You mean he ain't eaten? In three days? You didn't give him no food?"

"Give? I ain't in the business of giving away food, boy. Especially to Orientals. Another Chinaman'll happen along here any day, I s'pose. They can take care of him."

"What if one don't, though?"

Mr. Miller fixed me with an out-of-all-patience stare.

"T'ain't no concern of mine," he drawled slowly. "Them's words you oughta start learning yourself, boy. 'Specially if you aim to track down Ezra Bishop. You go after him lookin' for trouble, you'll find it for certain. Now. You buyin', or you leavin'?"

There was sure enough a lot swirling 'round in my heart and my head at that moment. I was pulled every which sort of way. There was the boy out there, alone. There was my girl Sarah, getting whipped away from me. There were all my own fears and doubts and loneliness piled up inside me. And as always, above all else there was my mama and papa. I tried to figure best as I could what it is they would have me do.

I reached into my satchel and pulled out a ten dollar note.

"I'm buying, sir. What you got in the way of ready-to-eat foods?"

When I stepped back outside, my satchel hung heavier on my shoulder. A tin canteen with a screw-top lid was slung over my other shoulder, full of water, seeing as I had plenty more walking ahead of me. I went over to the boy still sitting against the wall. He looked up at me, scared and breathless. I knelt down and held out a biscuit.

He looked at it, then back up at me. His lips were white and cracked. I wondered if he'd had any water all the while he'd been sitting here. I was darn near certain Mr. Miller hadn't brought him any.

"Go on," I said. "Take it." I pulled the canteen off my shoulder and shook it so he could hear the water, then unscrewed the lid and put it on the ground next to him. He gave me one more wide-eyed look, then snatched the canteen and gulped at it noisily. He stopped to take a breath and wiped his mouth with his sleeve, then timidly reached out and took the biscuit from my hand. It was gone in three bites and washed down with more water. He looked at me, panting. I smiled.

"Better?"

He blinked at me.

Then he wiggled and pulled something out of his pants pocket and held it in his open palm. I squinted down at it. It was a small carving, like a little statue, made out of some kind of shiny black rock. It was in the shape of a bird, a long kind of bird like a crane or a heron, but it was small enough that he could've hid it if he'd closed his hand.

He held it out to me and said a few scratchy words in Chinese. I didn't know a lick of what he was saying, but I could tell from the sound of his voice and the look in his eyes that he was asking me a question.

I shrugged my shoulders helplessly.

He said the words again, more insistently this time, stretching to hold the bird closer to me so I could see it better.

"I'm sorry," I said, shaking my head. "I don't know what you're saying. You speak any English?"

He just blinked at me again, then pursed his lips and slid the little black bird back into his pocket. I thought I could see tears welling up in his eyes.

"Okay," I said softly. "No English. Well, I'll go ahead and talk anyways. I'm heading that way," I said, pointing south toward Rock Island. "You're welcome to come with me. I got some food and I'm heading toward bigger towns. Towns with more Chinese, likely. You wanna come?"

There was no flicker in his face, no sign he understood a plum word of what I'd said. I stood up and screwed the lid back on the canteen.

He sat stone still, looking up at me. I reckon I ain't never seen no one looking scareder than that Chinese boy sitting there all alone. I held out a hand, down toward him.

"Come on. There ain't nothing for you here."

I could see he was frozen. When you ain't got nowhere to go, I s'pose it's easy to stay right where you are, no matter how awful.

"Come on. It'll be all right. You'll see."

I saw the decision come together, right there in his eyes. His eyebrows crinkled for just a second, like he was getting ready to jump off a moving stagecoach, and then he reached up and grabbed hold of my hand. I pulled him up and got another biscuit outta my satchel while he beat the dust off his britches.

I handed him the biscuit and he did some sort of nod or bow that looked an awful lot like a "thank you."

"Don't mention it," I said, sticking out my hand. "My name's Joseph Johnson."

He just blinked at me and held his head way back like he thought I was gonna hit him.

"Joseph," I said louder, thumping myself on the chest. Nothing.

"Joseph!" I repeated, poking myself with a finger.

"Joseph!" Then I held my hands out to him, waiting for him to say his name.

The kid just blinked some more and then frowned.

"Look. We got a ways to go, you and me. We gotta at least be able to call each other something." I reached out and grabbed his hand. He flinched but didn't yank it back. I pulled his hand up and held it against my chest. "Joseph. Get it? Joseph?" I dropped his hand and then pressed my own up to his chest. I could feel his heart beating through his thin black shirt, fast and hard like a scared rabbit's. I curled my eyebrows into question marks. "You? Huh? You?"

The kid just stood there looking at me with his pounding heart and blank face.

I dropped my hand with a sigh.

"All right. Well, let's get a move on."

A nervous storm brewed in my belly. My mission had already been a tough one, when I only had myself to worry about. Adding a Chinese boy who didn't know a word of English to the mix weren't gonna make it any easier. But I knew with a certainty that I'd done what my mama and papa woulda wanted me to.

I turned up the road and started walking. The Chinese boy fell in line, a step behind me.

We walked off together to find the devil who had my horse.

CHAPTER 4

We trudged along for hours without neither of us saying a word. Once we'd passed the few buildings of Wenatchee proper, the rocky dirt road mostly wound through sageland and orchards and around boulders near as big as houses. The blue water of the Columbia River sparkled off to our left, and pine-dotted hills rose up on our right. Here and there we'd see a cabin or a lean-to where someone was trying to make a go of homesteading. A couple of folks passed us on horseback, and we had to get out of the way of one wagon, but for the most part we had that wide-open country to ourselves. It was warm for October, and I wiped at the sweat on my forehead from time to time.

My companion insisted on staying a good five or six steps in back of me. The few times I stopped so he could catch up, he just stopped, too, and looked sideways at me until I got to moving again.

Then the road took a sharp turn to the right, straight up into the layered hills that I knew would take us over Colockum Pass and to the town of Ellensburg on the other side. It sure looked like a lot of hills and a lot of climbing, but there was nothing to do but put our heads down and start on up.

The road through Colockum Pass felt even steeper going up than I remembered from coming down it the previous spring with my papa. Whether my silent partner liked it or not, we had to struggle a fair bit together, helping each other up and catching each other when we'd slip. He seemed a little less scared by my touch each time.

We grunted our way up the mud track for who knows how many hours, and by the time the sun was near to setting, we still had hill after hill lined up in front of us. Looking back down the way we'd come, though, the river sure enough looked far off and small, so I knew we'd done some good traveling.

The evening chill was already in the air, and dark was coming on quick. I reckoned it was time for making camp. At the top of a little rise, out on a point overlooking the whole great river valley, I spied a little dry protected spot, tucked nice and neat under a big old rock overhang from the cliff above. There was a ring of stones on the ground and black soot on the rock ceiling, so I knew I weren't the first to find it.

I led my nameless partner over and dropped my satchel in the beat-down dirt under the overhang.

"This is it," I said. "Home sweet home." He looked at me with his unreadable face, still breathing hard from the last hill. "Let's get us some wood."

I walked off into the underbrush and scattered small pines, looking for good burnin' wood. My body was already starting to shiver, and I was eager as anything to get a good blaze going. Coming back into our camp, teetering under a load of wood, I noticed right off that the boy was gone. I dropped the wood and looked around and there he came, stumbling out of the fading light with his own armload of wood.

He dropped it with a clatter where I'd dropped mine.

"Good," I panted with a nod. "More."

By the time we had a big enough pile to last the night, stars were starting to blink above us, and the sky was that dark kind of purple just before black. Together we hoisted a nice big log with a flat side over to our camp and set it so we could sit on it. Then I pulled the matches I'd bought from Mr. Miller out of my satchel and set to getting a fire going.

Soon there was crackling wood and cheerful yellow light and a more-than-welcome warmth from the crooked ring of stones. I found a seat on the log and the Chinese boy sat on the other end, as far as he could from me without falling off. The overhang was a cozy little shelter, safe from most of the breezes that blew through from time to time, and the stone wall behind us bounced the heat of the fire back at us so we was pretty much warmed from both sides. We sat for a while, chewing at the apples and strips of jerky I took from my satchel.

I don't know why I started talking. I guess maybe there's just something about sitting by a fire that makes a fella wanna talk.

"I'm going to get my horse back," I said, staring into the twisting flames. The boy's head snapped up and he looked over at me sideways. "Her name's Sarah. She's a nine-year-old filly. A red-and-white paint with a notch in one ear—prettiest pony you ever saw. Fast as blazes, too. She's half Indian pony, so she's got some spirit, but she ain't nothing but perfect with me. She turns 'fore I even have to tell her. Mama always said it was like we shared a heart, Sarah and me."

The fire popped and hissed. Out somewhere in the darkness beyond the firelight, an owl hooted. The boy took another bite of his apple. Living with Mr. Grissom I hadn't had a soul to talk to, and I could sure enough feel all those dammed-up words crowding to get outta me.

"Pa got her for me when I was four, when she was just a yearling, so's we could grow up knowing each other. Had me up on her right away. I was riding her bareback by the time I was five, and jumping fences when I was nine." I looked over at him. "I don't suppose you ever had a horse?"

He just swallowed nervously and kept his eyes on the fire.

I got up to throw another log onto the fire. I stood for a second by the woodpile, looking up at the sky. Stars were glittering here and there, with more sparking up all the time.

"My little sister said a funny thing about stars," I said, sitting back down. "She'd heard that some Indians think the stars are the campfires of our ancestors. That once we die, we go up to join 'em and get a fire of our own." I knew my voice had gotten awful quiet, but since I was talking to a person who didn't speak a word of English, I figured speaking up wasn't all that important. "When you die, you ain't got no matches or nothing with you, so she figured the fires must already all be lit by God, just waiting to welcome folks and give 'em a warm place in heaven to sit. She always wondered which one was for her." I felt a little smile, just a little one, teasing at the corners of my mouth. But at the same time, I felt a hot wetness in my eyes I tried to blink away. "So we'd—so we'd always look up and pick out ours. We'd pick out which one was our campfire, waiting for us in heaven."

My voice broke off and I turned away, ashamed at the tears on my cheeks. But once those words started coming, it was like there was no stopping 'em.

"It's funny. Pa and I made it all the way down this pass, with the mud and the switchbacks and the hairpin turns, dragging a log to slow us the whole way and fighting for every foot. And then the hill that kills him up over at Old Mission is plum nothing. Just a little slope, really, wouldn't hardly take your breath to walk up it. But the wagon just got a little away from us and that wheel got stuck and like that he throws me clear and I'm rolling down the hill and he's stuck under that cursed wagon." I sniffed and wiped at my nose. "It ain't fair. Ain't fair for him to go like that, after all we'd gone through to get there. Ain't fair for him to go when I ain't got nothing or no one else left. Nothing but my horse." The tears were back and more than I could hold on to. I hid my face but I couldn't keep my shoulders from shaking, and my breathing was loud and sniffling. I don't know what it was that got to me right then. Maybe it was just all of it— the cold and the hunger and the all-aloneness, and shot right through it was the feeling of my Sarah getting farther and farther away. I s'pose sadness can sometimes be a storm that's easy to get lost in.

I was surprised when I felt something touching my shoulder. I looked through blurry eyes and saw that the boy had slid on over 'til he was right up against me. His face had that same blank expression but I thought I could see, mixed up in it, a little bit of something else. Understanding, maybe. He reached 'round, just once, and gave my back a little pat.

Then he started talking.

Quiet, at first. So quiet I could barely hear him. That Chinese talking came on in a scratchy whisper, shy and stumbling as it got started. He talked into the fire, and the flames flickered in his eyes as his voice got more strength to it. His words were like a song I didn't know the tune of, full of quick turns and drops.

I just sat and listened, like he had for me. At some point I realized he was crying, but only with his eyes—there weren't no shake to his voice, no sniffle to his breathing. His tears came down silent like falling snow, and his talking never let up. I figured he must've had some words dammed up in him, too. I sure enough didn't know a word of what he was telling me, but I reckon it had to do with the same kind of stuff stuck inside me: family, and things that were lost, and having no place to call home. Maybe he was talking about his mama, however many thousands of miles away, or dead, even. Maybe he was talking about his pa, buried back in Wenatchee, or about some brother or sister he'd likely never see again.

He reached into his pocket and pulled out the little carving he'd shown me earlier, that shiny black stone bird. He held it out to me while he kept talking, and I took it careful, turned it over to look at it, then handed it back to him. He slid it back into his pocket and wiped at his cheeks with his sleeve.

I reached around him, just like he had to me, and patted him on the back. He looked at me with a serious face, then reached over and put his hand to my chest.

"Joseph," he said.

"What'd you say?"

"Joseph," he said solemnly, with a little nod. Then he grabbed my hand and pulled it up to his own chest. I could feel his heart beating, just like before, but it weren't beating scared like a rabbit's anymore.

"Ah-Kee," he said, thumping my hand soft against himself. "Ah-Kee."

"Ah-Kee," I repeated. He nodded and I nodded back, and then I smiled. I pulled my hand from his chest but left it held out in front of him. He looked at it, then understood and took it up in his own. We shook hands, sitting there shivering shoulder to shoulder on the mountainside with the campfires of our ancestors shining down on us.

"Pleased to meet you, Ah-Kee," I said.

CHAPTER 5

When we woke in the morning the world was crisp with thick white frost and our breaths came out as puffy clouds. We'd spent most of the night curled up against each other as close to the fire as we could get. It was too cold to stretch out or lay down, and we kept having to take turns getting up to put more wood on.

I woulda killed for some bacon or eggs, but we had to make do with another biscuit each and some salt pork that was so hard from the cold that my jaw hurt three chews into it. Ah-Kee didn't complain, though, and we were back on the road up the mountain before the sun was all the way clear of the horizon.

We only passed one other set of travelers on the trail that morning. It was a homesteader family, laboring their way down with a brake log tied off the back of their wagon. The man took enough time to tip his hat and give us a howdy, but his wife took one look at Ah-Kee and curled her lip and they went on their way without saying another word. Otherwise the mountain was ours, with its brown fall grass and endless uphill climbing and forever-views of the Columbia laid out like a ribbon way down below us. The higher we got the more pine trees started crowding around us and soon we left the bare sageland behind and were in honest-to-goodness forest.

'Round about what felt like noon I stopped at a level spot, my breath coming hard and my forehead sweating in spite of the chill in the air. Ah-Kee was panting, too, and looked just as ready to stop as I was. I dropped my satchel right in the dirt and stood there catching my breath.

"Lunchtime, Ah-Kee?" I asked. He cocked his head at me. I brought pretend food to my mouth and did some theatrical chewing. Understanding flashed on Ah-Kee's face. For the first time ever I saw him truly smile, and he nodded eagerly. Your belly knows every language when it's hungry and there's food to put in it, I s'pose.

I smiled, too, then pointed with a thumb back behind me.

"I gotta, well, relieve myself." Ah-Kee must've got the gist of what I said 'cause he just nodded and made his own way off into the brush in the other direction. Once off the road I kept going farther for privacy's sake, through the bushes and bunches of grass that grew under the pines. All in the air was the crisp smell of fall blended with pine and sage. The sunlight was a flat pale yellow, not the sharp brightness of summer. It was a fine afternoon, really.

I was finished with my business and buttoning up my britches when I heard the first growl.

I froze, hands on my unbuckled belt. Whatever'd made that growl sounded close. And big.

All the peace I'd felt from the sunlight and sage and scenery dried up like nothing.

Real slow-like I turned my head toward the sound.

Standing there, not more than fifty yards away, was the biggest bear I'd ever seen in all my days.

It was standing, just on the other side of a small draw. And it was looking right at me.

I was glad I'd just done my business, or I reckon I'da ruined my pants right then and there.

It weren't just its size that scared me, nor its uncomfortable closeness to me, but its silver-tipped brown color and the hump on its back.

"Grizzly," I whispered to myself and any angels close enough to hear and help. I'd heard that all the grizzlies had been hunted out of these hills, but evidence to the contrary was fifty yards away, full of rippling muscle and teeth. There was at least *one* grizzly left in the Colockum. And I'd found him.

The monstrous bear chose that moment to stand up, rising high on his back legs to get a better look at me. He was taller than a horse, easy. Heck, he looked taller than me sitting *on* a horse. If my pounding heart hadn't been stuck in my chest, I'm pretty sure it would've leapt right out and skittered away down the mountain.

All I could think of was my papa's pistol, all the way back in my satchel on the road.

The bear let out another growl that ended in something a lot more like a roar, then dropped to all fours and took a few running steps toward me, down the far slope of the little canyon between us.

I took right off running, jangling belt and all, stumbling

through the brush back toward Ah-Kee and a pistol that suddenly seemed terribly far away and awfully small.

I could hear the bear crashing behind me, down through the canyon and up the nearer side—it sure enough thundered, grunting and stomping and cracking branches like a train going through those trees. It sounded like a monster was on my tail, and coming fast.

I wanted to scream in terror, but my lungs were too busy sucking wind.

Crack! went a limb behind me, then only steps later another *snap!* and already the second sounded closer to me than the first. That grizzly was a ways back but gaining fast.

I came 'round the last bend and saw at last the road in front of me, and my satchel lying on it.

"Ah-Kee!" I finally managed to scream. "Run! There's a—" My warning was cut off when I fell suddenly, smashing into the ground with a thud that chased the breath right out of my lungs. I tried to jump up but my limbs wouldn't cooperate. I felt sharp talons scraping at my legs.

The bear's got me! The thought stabbed into my heart like a black dagger, and I knew all was lost. I was gonna die there on that mountain and I'd never see my sweet Sarah again. The grizzly had caught me and grabbed hold of my legs and was opening its terrible jaws to tear me into bloody pieces. I flopped over onto my back with my eyes squeezed shut against the horror and hollered out my dying scream.

There was a split half-breath of a moment—and then I

realized I could still hear the bear roaring and raging toward me. Closer . . . but not on me yet. I looked down and saw the reason for my falling: my unbuckled pants had come down around my ankles. There weren't no talons—the brush and branches on the ground were scraping and poking at my exposed legs and rear end.

I cursed, forgetting in my fear how my mama looked upon such language. I yanked my britches up and stumbled to my feet and took off again, holding my pants up with one hand. That grizzly was close enough now for me to hear each and every step it took behind me as I careened frantically through the trees toward my waiting pistol.

I slipped in a mud patch and took one more tumble but rolled to a stop right beside my satchel, my pants back down around my knees. Panting and bloody from my falls, I looked up and saw Ah-Kee come running out onto the road from the other side, his eyes wide at my fallen britches and his face full of questions.

"Bear!" I said, pointing and jumping to my feet with satchel in hand. His eyes followed my pointing just as the grizzly came lumbering out of the trees fifty feet away. Ah-Kee's mouth dropped open and his eyes got even wider. "Come on!" I shouted, yanking my pants up and grabbing him by the shirt as I ran past, dragging him along toward a big craggy boulder a little ways up the road. Behind us a vicious growl came rumbling low out of the bear's throat. I looked back and saw it charging up the hill behind us. That beast was so big and burly it looked like a raging, toothy stagecoach.

The boulder was taller than us and perfect for climbing, with cracks and ledges for fingers and toes, and Ah-Kee and I made short work of getting to the top. Just in time, too—when we scrambled up and jumped to our feet, the grizzly was right there, standing at the bottom, looking up at us with its head the size of a whole hog. He roared a ferocious roar that hurt my ears and shook my heart, showing us his mouthful of deadly looking teeth.

We were far from being out of danger. The top of that boulder was flat enough but small, barely enough for the two of us to stand on. We had to cling to each other to keep from falling off. And it weren't tall enough, neither; if that bear got it in his mind to stand on his back legs and swing his huge paws, I was pretty sure he'd have no problem shredding our legs to bloody bits from the knees down. It was only a matter of time until Ah-Kee and I were lunch for a bear.

I yanked the pistol out of my satchel. Its silver barrel flashed in the sunlight like sure-enough salvation. I knew a pistol wasn't likely to do much more to a grizzly than make it mad, but I didn't see no other options showing themselves. If I was lucky, from this close, I figured I might be able to get a bullet right into his eye. I hoped that would be enough to kill him, or at least hurt him enough to drive him away.

The bear circled 'round the boulder, no doubt looking for a way to get us down. Ah-Kee and I spun together, keeping the bear in our sight. I checked the chamber to make sure the pistol was loaded. The brass ends of six .45 caliber bullets gleamed up at me. My hands were shaking something fierce. I'd shot the pistol plenty, but only at rabbits and pheasant and the like; never before had I faced anything like the eight hundred pounds of mean hungry that was prowling below me now.

Ah-Kee shouted something frantic in Chinese. I looked up quick from the gun and saw the bear had stood up. He snarled his lips and swiped with his knife-blade claws at me. I dodged too slow, and those bear claws raked across my right leg, tearing straight through my pants. A searing hot pain shot up to my brain and I felt hot sticky blood drip down into my boots.

I cried out and almost lost my balance, but Ah-Kee tightened his grip on my body and kept me from toppling down into the bear's waiting maw. We scooted as far back as we could on the boulder and the bear dropped to all fours, circling around again to find a way to reach us. Our time on that rock—and our time on Earth, for that matter—was running out quick. I tried to calm my heart and steady my hands as I clicked the pistol closed and wrapped my finger 'round the trigger. Holding that pistol in my hand, I risked closing my eyes for just a moment, feeling its familiar grip tight against my sweaty palm. I remembered the feel of Papa's strong hands on my shoulders, his voice soft in my ear, as he taught me to shoot it. *Relax your shoulders but keep your arms strong, son. It's gonna kick at you when you fire, so you best be ready. Hold it steady with both hands. There you go. Breathe straight and easy. And remember you don't pull the trigger with your finger . . . You let all your air out slow and soft and then squeeze easy with your whole hand. Tell me when you're ready, son, then go ahead and shoot."* I felt a queer kind of peace settle into me. With Papa's voice in my ear, even just the memory of it, I figured I could do just about anything.

I opened my eyes. The bear had circled and was just off to my side. I turned, almost calm, and brought the gun up, steady in both hands. I relaxed my shoulders but kept both arms strong. I ignored the throbbing pain in my leg and kept my breathing straight and easy.

The bear rose up again, bringing his head near even with my feet. His two eyes, small on such a huge head, glared up at me, black and cold. His fangs, bared and glistening, shined white and deadly sharp. I sighted down the pistol barrel, lining it up with the bear's right eye. He roared, a heart-busting fearful sound, but I held on to Papa's voice, and neither my breathing nor my steady arms faltered.

"I'm ready, Papa," I whispered, and let all my air out slow and soft. The whole world went quiet except for my heart beating in my ears, and my hand tightened 'round the trigger.

My arms jerked down hard, but it weren't from the kick of the pistol. There'd been no kick, 'cause there'd been no shot. Just before the trigger had come back that last fatal hair's width, Ah-Kee had struck out, smacking my arms down.

"What're you doing, Ah-Kee?" I shouted. He was hollering, too, tugging on my sleeve and screaming Chinese in my ear. "It's the only way," I said roughly, figuring he was worried about making the bear madder than it already was. I jerked my arms free from his grip and raised the gun again. "I think I can get him through the eye." The bear swiped at us again with those grim black claws, but from where he was, he couldn't quite reach, and his paw whistled through the air just short of our legs.

I squared the pistol sights once more on the grizzly's murderous eye. Ah-Kee was still yammering at me in Chinese, his voice high and frantic. I blocked the sound out of my mind and tried to find my papa's voice again as I kept that pistol barrel steady on the bear's eye.

Again Ah-Kee swept my arms down, stopping my shot, and I turned toward him in anger 'til I saw that he was pointing at something. Something down the road, at the edge of the trees the bear had chased me out of moments before.

There were two of 'em. Grizzly cubs. They were standing up, looking our way, not much bigger than dogs.

The grizzly at our heels weren't a *he* at all. It was a mama.

I looked at Ah-Kee, knowing what he meant. He didn't want me to shoot the bear. Because she was a mama. He didn't want to make those cubs orphans.

He stopped shouting and we stood there a moment, looking into each other's eyes. His were serious, and urgent. We were both breathing hard.

"I'm sorry, Ah-Kee," I said finally. "I got to. It's what's got to be done."

Ah-Kee shook his head. He said a few words, quiet but firm, in his foreign tongue. His wide eyes were full and glistening.

"I'm sorry," I said again, shaking my own head. He let go of my arms and I swallowed, steeling myself one more time for what I had to do. The bear had moved a few feet more to my left, and I pivoted to follow her. "You can look away if you want to, Ah-Kee," I said, bringing the pistol up.

The mama bear stood up, both paws on the boulder. Those black claws, longer than my fingers, scraped at the rock. Her eye looked up wetly at me, and I put it right in the sights of my papa's pistol and got my heart ready to send a bullet into her brain.

But then, just before I pulled the trigger, I realized something was missing.

There weren't no one screaming Chinese in my ear. I didn't feel a scared body pressed up against mine, or hands holding on to my shoulders, or breathing in my ear.

I looked over my shoulder just in time to see Ah-Kee lower himself from the boulder top, and hop down onto the ground.

CHAPTER 6

My heart dropped down to my feet.

"*Ah-Kee what in the ever-loving world do you think you're—*" I hissed, but stopped, not wanting to alert the grizzly that Ah-Kee was on the ground with her, just on the other side of the boulder.

But there weren't no need for my caution.

Ah-Kee didn't scurry off, or try and hide, or any such thing.

Ah-Kee, arms at his sides and just as calm as you please, walked right around the boulder toward where that mama grizzly stood with her bloody claws and ready teeth and unshot eye, waiting to eat me.

And as he walked, he was talking. Nice and easy, low and calm, Ah-Kee was talking to that bear in Chinese.

When he rounded the corner, the bear's head snapped over to look at him. I think she was as surprised as I was.

She dropped to all fours and took a fast angry step toward him, a growl hard and hungry in her throat, where I guessed a sizable chunk of Ah-Kee would soon be.

But Ah-Kee just stopped where he was and kept on talking, his voice mellow like a cracklin' campfire. Like a river telling stories.

And that grizzly stopped, too. A few feet away from him, almost eye to eye with him, close enough no doubt to strike with those claws and bring his blood out.

I stood on top of that boulder, looking down on a mama grizzly and a Chinese orphan, a cocked pistol frozen in my hand.

The bear roared, a full and meaty roar with plenty of fierceness and fury in it—but the roar seemed to end in a kind of question mark. And she stood where she was. And Ah-Kee kept talking.

Then, as he talked, Ah-Kee reached with one hand into his shirt and pulled something out. I squinted to see. It was the carving, that little black bird. He held that stone bird out to the grizzly and told her all about it. And she stood there listening, sniffing at the wind and looking at the plum crazy boy in front of her.

I don't know if I breathed or swallowed for two whole minutes or for however long it took for Ah-Kee to tell his story to that angry mama grizzly.

But then he was done. He bowed to her, stiff and quick, and then walked across the road a bit, away from her babies. He climbed a few steps up the bank on the side of the road and sat down, then put his hands on his knees and looked at the bear.

I doubt whether anyone had ever stood before that big old grizzly and talked to her. But I sure reckon no one ever stood in front of her and talked to her in Chinese. I don't know what that bear was thinking, or what she was feeling. But she stood there looking at Ah-Kee for a minute, then she looked back up at me on the boulder, standing there stupidly and still pointing a gun at her. Then she grunted, and growled kinda to herself, and she walked down the road and back to her waiting cubs. They scampered forward to meet her, and together the three of them walked off into the trees.

I stood there for a second, catching my breath and collecting my wits, then I finally lowered the gun and uncocked the hammer.

I looked over at Ah-Kee. He looked up at me, his face expressionless.

"That was the dumbest thing I ever seen somebody do," I said in wonder. "And it was the bravest, too." A Chinese boy, thousands of miles from home, talking face-to-face with a mama grizzly to keep her cubs from becoming orphans. "I think my mama woulda liked you, Ah-Kee," I said.

He said a few words back to me in Chinese. I cocked my head at him. He smiled, the biggest smile I'd seen crack his face, and pointed up at me, but a bit lower than my face. I looked down.

In all the excitement, I'd lost track of my britches. They'd fallen down again around my ankles. My drawers, too. I was standing there on top of a rock for all the world to see, with a pistol in my hand, naked as the day I was born from the waist down. A cool draft blew through my legs.

I heard Ah-Kee laugh for the first time as my face turned redder than a turkey's wattle and I rushed to yank up my pants.

We camped that night just over the top of Colockum Pass. It was a fine feeling when we got to the top of our last uphill climb and saw the road heading down in front of us, rolling around bends into the great, spread-out valley below us. There were a lot more trees on this side of the mountains, and I could only see the road here and there through the timber until it disappeared.

Somewhere down there was the town of Ellensburg, where I hoped Ezra Bishop was gonna hold for a while so I could catch him. I scanned the forested hills below hungrily, hoping just maybe to see in the distance a man on a horse, leading a string of ponies that included a beautiful red-and-white paint with a notched ear. Everything was still, though, and quiet, and the whole landscape was falling into shadow as the sun got ready to set. My Sarah was nowhere to be seen. Part of me wanted to call, to holler her name with all the air in my lungs and let it echo down to wherever she was. I just knew that if she heard me call, she'd break any rope and brave any whip to get to me. But I knew it was no use. I sighed. At least I didn't see any grizzlies.

I turned to Ah-Kee as he stepped up to where I was. "That's it," I said, sweeping my arm at the view before us. "No more *up*." He leaned down with his hands on his knees to catch his breath, and nodded. I think he understood. A wind was starting to blow and it was sure enough *cold*, pushing right through the threads of my clothes and bringing gooseflesh out all over my body.

We found a spot between two big boulders for camp. There weren't much talking this time, but right from the start we sat up against each other, both happy for the warmth of the other. The grizzly had left four deep, raw cuts in my leg that throbbed with a constant pain. I washed my leg off as best I could with water from our canteen, but I didn't have no bandages or even cloth to wrap it with. I had to just hope I wouldn't get no infection.

In the morning Ah-Kee shook me awake. I'd been lost in an uneasy dream that was half memory, with the biting sound of a shovel and the smell of fresh dirt and Papa standing with his arm around me, his body shaking with quiet sobs. It took me a confused moment to realize it was Ah-Kee shaking me and not Papa, but I was glad to let the sad cloud of that dream get blown out of my mind by the morning chill.

His voice was half whisper, half shout and sounded more excited than scared. I blinked my eyes and looked around to see what he was all agitated about.

Snow. All around us, covering the rocks and the trees and the brush. Not a lot, but enough to know it was snow and not just a heavy frost. It was even on our shoulders and knees. I brushed it off and couldn't help but let a smile onto my face. I was shivering something fierce, but I'd always loved snow. It was still falling, but barely, just little flakes here and there dancing lightly down to the ground.

"Angel feathers," I said quietly, watching it fall. Ah-Kee looked at me. "That's what my sister called it. Katie." Saying her name out loud like that, after so long, made me want to smile and cry at the same time. It made me feel a whole different kind of alone. "When there was snow like this in the morning, I used to say it looked like sugar, like the whole world had gotten candied overnight. But she insisted it was feathers from the wings of angels, flying around at night watching over people." Ah-Kee sat there and listened with his solemn eyes. I blew my breath out in a foggy cloud. "Let's stoke the fire and eat some grub and hit the road."

Going down a mountain was sure enough easier than battling up one and we made good time all morning, barely slowing down to eat our lunch when the sun was straight overhead and our bellies were growling. It was the last food from my satchel, giving me one more reason to want to get to Ellensburg as fast as we could.

We were rounding a bend through an especially thick part of the forest when I stopped short and held out an arm to stop Ah-Kee. I'd heard something, something out in the trees away from the road, but I wasn't sure what. I prayed that it weren't another grizzly, looking for one last meal before bedding down for the winter. At least I had my pants on this time.

I heard it again, and Ah-Kee did, too. We both tilted our heads in the same direction. The trees were so thick and close together that the road was almost dark.

There it was again, and now I was sure it was a voice. It sounded about fifty feet off the trail, out of sight through the underbrush. There were a few more low words and I realized it was a boy's voice, and he sounded like he was in distress. I noticed something else, too; I was pretty sure he weren't speaking English, and that he weren't speaking Chinese, either.

I walked off the road a few feet, keeping my ears sharp and my feet quiet. I could feel Ah-Kee following behind.

A calm in the breeze brought the tree rustling to a quiet, and I heard a whole sentence clear as day. It was definitely a boy's voice, and he sounded hurt. I hesitated. Walking into what could be danger ain't never the smartest idea, and I had a horse to catch. But I knew Mama and Papa would never abide walking by when another soul needed help.

Then I heard another voice. It was a girl's, and younger. She sounded little, and she sounded afraid. I didn't wait, but charged straight off through the woods toward the voices.

I pushed through brush and ducked under branches and then came out into a little clear spot. As I broke through the last branches the voices stopped.

I stumbled to a halt. As Ah-Kee crashed up behind me, my eyes took in the scene before me.

It was Indians.

Two of 'em. A boy, older and taller than me, his bare arms taut with muscles. And a girl, five or six years old, with her arms around him and a terrified look on her face.

The boy's eyes narrowed. He bared his teeth like a wolf and snarled a word low and mean in his native tongue. A shaft of sunlight through the treetops gleamed on the long knife blade held in his hand as he ducked into a crouch and lunged toward me.

CHAPTER
7

I jumped back from the boy with the knife, bumping into Ah-Kee. Our legs got tangled and we both tumbled to the ground. I started crab-crawling away, Ah-Kee scrambling right beside me, our feet skittering and sliding in the pine needles on the forest floor until I backed right into a big ol' tree trunk and came to a sudden and painful stop.

My hand darted to my satchel for the pistol but stopped when I saw that the Indian wasn't getting any closer. In fact, he was lying on the ground, right where I'd last seen him. The girl was standing over him, looking at me and Ah-Kee with big scared eyes.

I took a few deep breaths to calm my heart and then rose slow and careful up to my feet. Ah-Kee stood by my side. The Indian was holding his leg with both hands and wincing, his face screwed up in pain.

"You're hurt," I said, taking a step forward. He growled a sharp string of words at me and rose to one knee, swiping the knife in the air. His eyes flashed with a red-hot angry fire that stopped me cold, but then his face went pale, and he clutched at his leg and almost toppled over again. It was clear as anything that he was in a heckuva lot of pain.

"It's all right," I said, keeping my voice calm and quiet. "We don't mean you no harm." I slid the satchel off my shoulder and set it down, then took a small step toward him with my hands open and held out so he could see they were empty.

His body tensed, but there was no more cursing or slashing with the knife.

"What you got going on here?" I asked, taking two more steps closer and squinting at his leg. I gasped when I saw it.

"Good Lord Almighty," I breathed. "You done broke your ankle." I could see it easy, even from a few feet away. His ankle was swollen up like a watermelon, and the skin all around it was stained with dark purple bruises. His foot dangled, twisted at an unnatural angle. I couldn't imagine the pain he was in.

His eyes were still on me, but they held a little less raw fury than they had a moment before. I held his gaze and nodded, then pointed at his mangled ankle. "That's bad," I said. "Real bad." He blinked but said nothing.

I took another step toward him and he said something quick to the girl crouched at his side. She sprang to her feet and started backing away across the clearing toward the trees and underbrush at the other side.

"No," I said, taking a step back. "Don't run. We'll leave you be."

I took another backward step and the girl rushed back to his side, wrapping her arms tight around his waist and looking at me with fearful eyes. They were big and round and shiny wet. Just like my sister Katie's had been when she'd been scared.

I hesitated.

That boy was not getting anywhere with the shape his ankle was in.

I blew all my breath out. I knew I couldn't just walk away and leave them like that. Mama and Papa would have never allowed it.

But that Indian's knife wasn't looking any friendlier.

My mind raced, looking for what to do next, and words from my mama came back to me: *There ain't no problem between people so big that it can't be solved by folks sitting down and talking about it.* Mama was generally right about anything that really mattered, but I wasn't sure if that particular piece of wisdom would work if the folks sitting down didn't speak the same language.

But then I remembered Ah-Kee and the bear. And I figured if a grizzly can be calmed by listening to a bunch of Chinese, there must be something to it.

So I sat down. Right there in the dirt. Quick, before the girl could disappear. And I started talking.

"We're just traveling down the road," I began, "and we heard you talking over here. My name is Joseph, and this here is Ah-Kee. We're heading to Ellensburg, coming from Wenatchee."

The Indian boy blinked, listening. I made my voice real casual, like we was just talking over bread and butter at a church picnic. The girl was watching me, too, real careful.

"I'm after a man who bought my horse from another man who had no right to sell her. Her name is Sarah and she's as fine a horse as any you'll ever come across. She means—" I stopped, surprised at how quick my emotion had come up. I swallowed it down and kept on going in my easy, friendly voice. "She means the whole world to me. And there ain't nothing I won't do or nowhere I won't go to get her back."

The boy looked wary but a whole lot calmer.

"I can see you broke your ankle there," I said, gesturing at it. "We don't have any food to offer, and as far as I know neither one of us is a doctor, but I reckon between us we can help you get wherever it is you need to get to, so long as it's not too far."

I knew that Indian probably didn't understand a plum word of what I said. But I reckon my mama was right after all; he could sure enough tell that Ah-Kee and me didn't mean no harm.

He sat there thinking for a second, then he slid his knife into a leather holster on his belt and nodded. He said a few words at me and I don't know what they meant exactly, but they were clear enough, so I stood up and grabbed my satchel and walked over to where he was crouching. I helped him up to his feet.

Ah-Kee was hunkered down where we'd fallen at the edge of the clearing, watching us carefully. I put the Indian's arm over my shoulder so he could lean on me. The girl stood off a ways, watching us just as closely as Ah-Kee was.

"Come on, Ah-Kee," I said, beckoning him over with a hand. I could tell he wasn't so sure, but he walked on over and took the Indian's other side. "All right," I said, looking into the Indian's eyes, "where we going?"

He just looked at me, trying to understand. I swept a hand out, gesturing at the forest around us. "Which way?"

There was a flicker of understanding in his face and he spoke a few words to the girl, who gave him one more unsure look and then headed off through the woods, back toward the road. Ah-Kee and I followed her, the Indian limping between us.

Despite my calm voice, my heart was hammering in my chest. I was in the grip of an actual, real-life Indian. I could feel the power in his muscles, even hurt as he was. I knew that knife was still right there at his waist. In my mind I heard all the terrible stories that settlers told about the vicious Indians. If this Indian suddenly changed his mind and decided he wanted my scalp, he'd have it long before I got my papa's pistol out.

We stumbled our way down the road a fair piece, then the girl led us off on a well-worn trail that ran south. The Indian's weight was taking its toll on my back and shoulders, and Ah-Kee and I had to stop from time to time to rest and trade sides. We were heading up a steep little hill through a mix of sage and pine when I heard the first sounds: whooping and hollering and thundering hooves, coming from over the rise we were climbing. There was a wild sound to it. My heart wanted to slow down but the Indian caught a spark of new life when he heard it and picked up his pace considerable. The girl ran eagerly ahead and disappeared over the top, her black braids bouncing as she ran.

Ah-Kee leaned forward to look at me around the Indian we were carrying. He said a good long sentence to me, his voice tense and nervous.

"We'll be all right, Ah-Kee," I said, wishing I felt as confident about that as I sounded.

We topped the rise and stopped to catch our breath and take in the view.

Below us, on a flat piece of land surrounded by hills and drops in every direction, was a crazy buzzing circus of life. There was a scattered crowd of Indians, more than a hundred, easy. There were teepees and smoking fires and horses everywhere, with the Indians in clusters all around and in between. Kids ran to and fro, chasing each other and shouting and playing.

At the far side was a long, straight dirt track that had been worn into the landscape. I reckoned it was nearly a quarter mile long. A crowd of Indians was gathered at either end, and even from that distance I could hear them talking and yelling. Then, as I watched, the crowds fell silent. There was a waiting moment, then two Indians on horseback tore off from one end, racing down the track like the devil himself was at their heels. They were riding bareback, their bodies hugging their horses, their long hair whipping in the wind, and they slapped their horses to urge 'em on faster, faster. The crowds started hollering again, cheering and howling. Those horses flew with a wild speed, moving with their riders like they were one animal. It was sure enough something to see. When they reached the far end of the track, one just before the other, they slowed down to a trot, with one Indian raising his hands in triumph and screaming out a victory yell and the other dropping his head in defeat. The people crowded at each end either cheered or groaned, depending, I supposed, on which horse they'd picked to win.

"Well, Ah-Kee," I said, wiping at my sweaty forehead with my arm, "looks like we found ourselves an Indian horse race." I'd heard of these competitions before, and what big affairs they were for the Indians. Groups got together and might spend two days racing, betting piles of hides and blankets and knives on which rider would win. I never thought I'd see one myself. But with that hurt Indian between us, right down into it Ah-Kee and I went.

We were down the slope and halfway to the nearest tee-pee when three men came striding toward us. The little girl trailed behind them, running to keep up. Their faces were deadly serious as they stood before us, looking like they were carved out of dark stone.

The biggest one among them sported a strong nose and streaks of gray in his hair. He said a few words to us, short and curt. It didn't sound friendly.

I just looked at him, but the boy I was holding spoke up, answering with a lot of words. At one point he held his injured ankle out, showing the swelling and bruising. There was no reaction in the older man's face, but his eyes went from the boy's ankle, to my face, to Ah-Kee, then back to the boy. He nodded and turned with the other men to walk back to camp. With a gesture and a reassuring grunt from the boy, Ah-Kee and I followed with him.

Life was all a-bustle in the world between the teepees. Everywhere people were coming and going and laughing and calling to each other. Fires were smoking and babies were crying and the smell of strange foods wafted here and there. It was *alive* there in the Indian camp by the racetrack. We came to a teepee in the middle and a group of women rushed over. With a chattering and clucking they took the injured boy away from us and hurried him off into the teepee, leaving Ah-Kee and me standing there looking at each other.

The three men who'd led us into the camp stood before us, faces still unreadable. I tried to smile at them but it didn't seem to take, so I called it off. A crowd of Indians was growing around us, curious and whispering. Children peeked at us from behind their grown-ups.

"That was a good move, saving a chief's son like that," said a voice behind us. I turned and was surprised to see a white man there, sitting on a big cinnamon-colored horse. He was lean and tall and wore a buckskin jacket with a dangling fringe, and a battered brown cowboy hat up on his head.

"Sir?"

"That boy you brought in. He's the son of one of the chiefs here—Chief George. He was off scouting for deer with his sister. They were expected back last night, so you showing up with him today was quite a relief."

The man lowered himself off his horse with a squeak of saddle leather. He held out his hand, and I took it in a firm shake.

"The name's Strawn," he said.

"Jack Strawn?" I asked in disbelief.

The man cocked an eyebrow at me.

"We know each other?"

"No, sir. Well, you don't know me. But I sure enough heard of you." Jack Strawn was something close to famous around those parts. He was one of the first white men to come over Colockum Pass into the Wenatchee Valley, and had been just about everywhere doing just about everything—prospecting for gold, trapping furs, trading with Indians. He weren't a hero or a legend or anything, but it was just that everyone knew him, and I'd heard his name plenty of times the past few months at the trading post or from other homesteaders.

"Huh. Well, mostly good, I hope." He looked at Ah-Kee for a second, then back to me. "Where's your kin?"

I looked away from him, off at the hills, then back up into his eyes.

"It's just me and Ah-Kee," I answered. "We're coming from Wenatchee, heading to Ellensburg."

More Indians had gathered 'round us now, pulling in closer. The three older men—were they all chiefs? I wondered—were still standing there, watching us.

Mr. Strawn blew out a low whistle.

"That's quite a hike on foot, son. What you after in Ellensburg?"

"A man," I said. "Ezra Bishop."

There was a dark murmur from the Indians around us. There was no mistaking the quick flame of anger that my words sparked among them. Ezra Bishop, it seemed, was a name they knew. And didn't like one bit.

Jack Strawn licked his lips, and though his head was still and his body calm, I saw his eyes flash around at the Indians that surrounded us. They came back to me and when he spoke his voice was calm and measured but deadly serious.

"You a friend of Ezra Bishop, son?"

"Friend?" I answered. "No, sir. He has a horse that's rightfully mine, and I aim to catch him and get her back."

A smile broke across Mr. Strawn's face, and I saw his shoulders relax. He looked past me at the three Indian men and talked to them in their native tongue. A ripple of relief ran through the crowd at whatever it was that he said. He looked back to me.

"Not being a friend of Ezra Bishop's just made you a load of friends among these folks," he said.

"Why's that, sir?"

"Ezra Bishop left here this morning, after a day of horse racing and trading yesterday," Mr. Strawn said. "He left here with a few more ponies than he arrived with. A few more than he rightfully should have, probably. And they feel more than a little sore about it."

"He stole their horses?"

Jack Strawn pursed his lips and scratched at his neck.

"Ezra Bishop is purty good at avoiding any crimes that he can actually be called to account for. He's a slippery one. It's more like he swindled and lied and bullied, then left before anything could be done. Did he steal them ponies? I s'pose not. But he didn't exactly take 'em honest. Ain't the first time, neither."

I thought of the way I'd seen Mr. Bishop whispering with Mr. Grissom, then waiting 'til I was gone before closing the deal and hightailing it out of there. I figured I knew exactly what Jack Strawn was talking about.

"He left this morning, sir? Early?"

"Afraid so. And he didn't trade any of his ponies away, so yours must still be with him."

"Did you happen to notice her, Mr. Strawn? She's a filly, a red-and-white paint. Half Indian."

His eyes widened.

"With a notch in her ear?"

"Yes, sir! You saw her, then?"

"Son, we *all* saw her. Your pony won Mr. Bishop several horses and a pile of furs. He paid a boy to ride her, and she took both races she ran in." He looked up and spoke some more Indian and a ripple of talk went through the crowd.

One of the chiefs took a step forward and spoke a few words. Jack Strawn nodded and turned to me.

"Chief George sure likes the idea of you taking that pony away from Mr. Bishop. He wishes you the best of luck."

I nodded, thinking. I looked at the horses all around, clustered here and there. I thought about Ezra Bishop leaving hours ago, on horseback and downhill. I thought about my own sore, tired legs. The hard truth gnawed at my belly. I'd never catch Mr. Bishop. Not on foot, anyway.

I looked up into Mr. Strawn's eyes.

"I appreciate that," I said. "But I don't need luck, sir. I need a horse."

Jack Strawn licked his lips.

"I reckon you do," he answered quietly.

I looked at the stern-faced Indians.

"What are my chances?" I asked him.

"Chances of what?"

"Of borrowing a horse."

"*Borrowing* a horse? From these folks? Hours after they been swindled by a crooked white man?" He smiled a sour smile and spit on the ground. "These folks have had enough taken from them by white men, and not just Mr. Bishop. I'd say you got a better chance of growing wings and flying after your horse."

At that moment, another race began over at the track. There was another storm of hollering and howling, more thunder of hooves. An idea shot into my brain like a flaming arrow. It was a desperate sort of idea, but I was in a desperate sort of situation.

"What if I won one?"

"Excuse me, son?"

"What if I won one? In a race." I patted my satchel. "I pick my horse. They can choose my competition. If I lose, they get my pistol."

Mr. Strawn shook his head. "A pistol ain't worth as much as a horse."

"Just to borrow, then. I lose, they keep my pistol for good. I win, I get the use of one of their horses. Just to Ellensburg."

Mr. Strawn pursed his lips.

"Well. There is an honest Indian agent in Ellensburg. The Indians trust him. I suppose you could leave the horse there." He nodded, then turned and talked again to the Indians. They had a little back and forth, and then he said to me, "You just got yerself a horse race, son."

CHAPTER 8

I stood looking at the group of horses the Indians had led me over to. They were crowded all close together, their legs tied to keep 'em from wandering. Jack Strawn had dismounted and stood by my side. Ah-Kee hung close, too—I couldn't imagine how confused he was as to what in the world was going on.

"Can you ride bareback?" Mr. Strawn asked me.

"Yes, sir. Since I was five."

"Good. All right, now, son. Pick your horse."

I walked around the herd, looking at their builds, their legs, their hooves, their eyes. I didn't want a horse huddling in the middle—I knew the boldest ones would be here, on the outside.

Halfway around, I saw him. A young stallion, strong-looking but on the small side. He was a deep red, with a black mane and tail. He stomped and pawed the ground, tossed his head. His muscles rippled and tensed. His eyes were aflame with high-burning energy.

I walked closer.

He rolled his eyes and snorted as I approached. The veins in his neck bulged like snakes.

"This one," I said.

The Indians laughed and said a few words to Mr. Strawn.

"I'd pick again, son. That one's barely broke. He's wild."

"Yeah," I said quietly, mostly to the horse. "But he's fast. And he's ready to run." I reached out to put my palm on the stallion's neck. Before I could touch him, he whinnied and started to shy away, but I kept my hand out steady and sure. I murmured to him, nice and easy. He blew out his breath and eyed me, ready to bolt. But I stretched just a bit farther, and he let my hand rest on his skin.

I could feel the stallion's heart, powerful and prideful, beating through my palm. I looked into his half-wild eyes. And he looked into mine. I thought of my Sarah, of her wildness and her speed and her true heart.

"This is the one," I repeated. And it was.

The horse track weren't nothing but a long straight dirt path, two horses wide, that had been worn into the landscape by who knows how many years of races.

I walked my stallion—struggling and rearing the whole way, much to the amusement of the gathered Indians—to the nearest end. A young Indian man, about eighteen or nineteen years old, had been picked to be my opponent. He was waiting, sitting atop a fine-looking black horse several hands taller than my own spirited stallion.

He sneered, his face full of scorn and arrogance, and talk-shouted a couple of unfriendly sounding sentences down at me. The Indians around me laughed.

"Good luck to you, too," I said. Only Mr. Strawn laughed.

Ah-Kee looked from me to my opponent. He looked down the track where I'd soon be racing. Realization lit up his face. He shouted at me in Chinese, then pointed down toward the crowd of waiting Indians at the finish. I nodded at him. His eyes went wide. Then he yelled a few more words and took off running, down toward the finish line. I smiled grimly. It'd be good to have a friendly face waiting for me at the end.

"Best mount up, son," Mr. Strawn said, pulling a pistol from his holster.

I shook my head, straining to keep the horse under control.

"Not 'til we're starting," I grunted. "This horse ain't gonna sit and wait once I'm on him."

Mr. Strawn nodded.

"Tell you what. You climb up when you're ready. I'll fire once you're up."

I took a few deep breaths, making sure the stallion was pointing in the right direction. I braced my whole body for what was coming. Then in one swift motion I bent down and yanked the hobbling rope free from the stallion's legs, grabbed hold of his mane, leaped up on his back, squeezed tight with my legs, and got a death grip with both hands on his black mane.

The stallion reared and shrieked.

Mr. Strawn fired his gun.

The Indian on his black mount shot away from us, hurtling down the dirt track.

I reached back and slapped at the stallion's flank with all my might.

And then we were off like we'd been shot from a cannon.

A crooked cannon. Set up sideways. And loaded awful clumsy.

I'd been right about that stallion's spirit and strength. But the Indians had sure enough been right about him being only half-broke.

The stallion ran, and ran some kind of fast, but he zigged and zagged on that dirt track. He kicked his hind legs out from time to time, trying to shake me. He broke stride here and there to buck me. We were moving in the right direction, but that black horse up ahead was getting farther ahead every second.

"Come on!" I shouted, risking letting go with one hand to slap at him again. "Come on!" I screamed again, slapping him harder and clinging tight with my knees to his bucking body as we careened down the trail. The horse picked up his pace and straightened out a bit but I could still feel more fight locked up inside him.

I rose up on shaking legs to put my mouth right up near that stallion's ears. He was running more or less flat-out now and I was in danger every second of toppling off his slippery hide. But I needed more speed, and I needed it now.

"Aiyiyiyiyieeee!" I hollered, a crazy shout just as wild and wordless as the stallion himself. And my heart beat hard and fierce, right into his heart, just like my mouth shouted into his ear. And my heart said: *Run! Run, horse! Show me your speed!*

The horse, and his heart, heard me.

His long stride straightened out. His muscles bunched and sang like a bowstring. His sloppy, jerking run boiled down into a hard, hot, pure sprint.

Sarah is a lightning-fast horse.

I'd never admit another horse was faster than her.

But, boy. That half-broke stallion—he'd make me consider it.

We gained on the cloud of dust that was our competition. My body rose and surged with the body of the stallion so that we moved like one breathing, flying thing.

Mr. Strawn had said I'd have to grow wings to catch up to Mr. Bishop. When that stallion really started running, I felt like I darn near had.

We were two lengths back. Then one. But the finish line with its crowd of watchers was close. I didn't know if we'd make it. The stallion's breaths were coming hard with each mighty spring of his legs. I breathed with him.

The stallion's nose came even with the black horse's flank. Then the Indian's knee. The Indian looked back in surprise, seeing my stallion drawing even with him. His face furrowed in determination and he doubled his shouting and slapping at his horse.

But it was no use.

There was no beating that stallion if he decided to win. Just like my Sarah.

When we rumbled past the cheering crowd, the head of the black horse was by my side. The head of the stallion was an easy arm's length out ahead.

Ah-Kee was jumping up and down, grinning and whooping.

I relaxed my wound-up body and let the stallion run itself out among the sage and pine 'til he was ready to turn around and walk panting back. The Indians crowded around me, smiling and patting at the stallion.

I'd won myself a horse, for a bit. But what I'd really won was a chance at getting my own horse back for good.

The Indians wanted us to stay for a while. They offered us food: smoked salmon, jerked buffalo meat, steamed roots. It sounded good to my belly.

But Ah-Kee wouldn't linger.

When he got the gist of what Mr. Strawn was telling us, back at the teepees, he shook his head emphatically and pointed at the road, yammering in Chinese.

Ah-Kee stepped up to Mr. Strawn and the few Indians standing with him. He pulled out that little carved black bird and held it out to them, asking his mysterious questions in his desperate voice, looking from face to face.

They shook their heads, confused. Ah-Kee's shoulders slumped and he returned the bird to his pocket. He looked at me with sad and beseeching eyes, then pointed again back at the road.

"All right," I said with a quick nod. "We'll keep moving."

"What's he after?" Mr. Strawn asked me.

"I don't know," I answered. "But he sure wants it bad."

"Just like you."

I looked up at Mr. Strawn. "Yeah. I s'pose so."

The Indians let me choose another horse to borrow—a bigger one this time, fit for two riders, and with a lot less wild in his veins. Jack Strawn walked with us back up to the main road toward Ellensburg, along with a few of the Indians, including the little girl that we'd met on the road. Her brother was nowhere to be seen, but I caught her peeking shyly at me from behind a few of the grown-ups. I smiled and gave her a little wave. Her face flushed, and she braved a small wave of her own back.

"I hope you find Mr. Bishop, son," Mr. Strawn said. "But I hope you don't."

"What do you mean, sir?"

Mr. Strawn spit into the dirt.

"You're a good boy. But Ezra Bishop is a very bad man. Dangerous. And if you do find him, you'll be finding a world full of trouble."

"All I want is to buy my own horse back."

"Yeah. You got more money than he paid for her?"

I looked away.

"No, sir. I've got less."

Mr. Strawn's eyes sharpened. It was a moment before he spoke.

"Son, I'm glad you didn't lose that pistol of yours. 'Cause if you end up buying your horse back from Mr. Bishop, it'll be with lead and not gold. You keep your wits about you."

I didn't have an answer for that. So I just shook Mr. Strawn's hand and clambered up onto the horse.

I looked down the road we were to travel. Somewhere down that road, not too terrible far away, was my sweet Sarah. With a pony under me I'd be able to cover ground fast. I could almost feel her neck against my cheek, almost hear the soft nicker she made when she saw it was me walking up to her. She was worth the trouble. She was worth the danger.

Then I turned, suddenly remembering Ah-Kee.

"Can you hold on to me with no saddle?" I asked. Ah-Kee just blinked up at me. "Well," I said, leaning down to offer him a hand up, "we're about to find out."

CHAPTER
9

Turns out Ah-Kee really couldn't hold on to me with no saddle.

Luckily we made it over the ridge and out of sight of Mr. Strawn and the Indians before he toppled off the first time, landing with a clumsy thud in a slippery smear of mud. At least I hoped it was mud. A lot of horses had come over that trail recently.

"You okay?" I called down. Ah-Kee barked a few angry words up at me, trying to wipe at the filth on his pants. I don't know if they have curse words in Chinese, but if they do I reckon Ah-Kee was saying 'em.

We got him back on the horse behind me, but it weren't another quarter mile before I was sitting alone on the horse again, looking down at Ah-Kee brushing himself off. It weren't the horse's fault. She was small and her back was slick, and Ah-Kee just kept bouncing and sliding sideways until he was getting a good close look at the ground. To his credit he always hopped up quick, though, and we were still making fairly good progress by my reckoning. I kept that pony moving as fast as I could while still keeping Ah-Kee on her back for a reasonable amount of time, and I could feel Ellensburg and my own horse getting closer.

It was after the fourth or fifth fall that Ah-Kee, still sitting on the ground with a scowl on his face, suddenly patted his pockets and gasped. His eyes went wide and he chattered up at me with high-pitched urgency in his voice.

"What's the matter?" I asked stupidly. He jumped up out of the dirt and dramatically patted his pockets, then held his hands out to me, open and empty. All at once I understood.

His little bird carving. My heart sank. I didn't know what it was, but I knew it meant a great deal to him.

I looked over my shoulder, up the trail we'd just come down.

"Heck, Ah-Kee, I'm sorry. But it coulda slipped out on any one of your falls. It could be anywhere." He must've gotten the sense of what I was saying because he shook his head vigorously and talked more forcefully, pointing back up the road. I saw his eyes start to glisten and I cursed, looking down the road toward Sarah and Ellensburg and then up the road toward all the muddy places where Ah-Kee had fallen. All I wanted was my horse back. That's all. And it seemed like everything was working together to keep me from her. But looking down at Ah-Kee, covered in mud with desperate tears in his eyes, I didn't have to think too hard to know what Mama and Papa would've had me do. I knew he didn't have nothing at all in this whole world but that little black bird.

I turned the horse around and held my hand down toward Ah-Kee.

"Come on," I said. "We'll find it. But then you gotta do some better hanging on so we can gain some ground."

We had no luck at the first spot we looked, but it was hard to tell whether it was because the bird wasn't there or because we just couldn't find one little black bird in all that brown mud. We didn't fare any better at the second spot, but it was just a patch of bare dry dirt so the looking was quicker.

The third spot was on a little hill spotted with scrubby shrubs. We both got on our hands and knees, crawling around and scanning the ground. I noticed every second how the sun got closer and closer to the horizon. I dearly wanted to avoid spending another night by a campfire, falling farther behind Ezra Bishop. If we could make it to town by sunset, I might have my horse back by dinner. I got a lump in my throat just thinking about it.

It was right about then that I saw the bird, the glossy blackness of its stone shining dimly under a prickly bush Ah-Kee had rolled into after hitting the ground.

"Ah-Kee! Ah-Kee!" I snatched the bird and spun around on my knees and held it out to him. He sprang at me like a mountain lion and grabbed the carving out of my hand. He rubbed it fiercely in his fingers for a moment like he was making sure it was really real, then looked at me and dove, wrapping me in a hug that knocked me back on my rear.

"All right, all right!" I laughed, struggling to breathe he was hugging me so tight. "Ease up, Ah-Kee." He gave me one last squeeze then sat back on his heels, looking at the little black bird. I thought for a minute, then pulled the white stone out of my pocket, the one I'd taken from Papa's gravesite.

I held the stone up so he could see it.

"Lookie here, Ah-Kee. We both keep something special in our pockets." I rubbed my thumb over the smooth face of the stone. "I suspect they're memories for both of us."

Ah-Kee said a line or two, his voice quiet but strong. I sure wished I knew what he was saying, 'cause it sounded good. Important, even. I think I probably got the gist, though.

"Yeah," I said. "It's good having a memory you can hold on to."

He held his bird out between his fingers, and I held my stone out, and we tapped them together, like we were doing a cheers before Thanksgiving dinner.

"All right," I said, standing up. "Now we got to make good time down this mountain, Ah-Kee. I'm after another memory I can hold on to, and she's likely waiting for me in Ellensburg. You gotta hold on to me up on that horse as tight as you did down here a second ago. You ready?"

Ah-Kee nodded and we helped each other up onto the waiting Indian pony. Ah-Kee's arms gripped tight around my middle and we took off down the mountain, racing the sun to the horizon.

We both held our memories tight in our hands, not trusting our pockets with something so important.

Ellensburg sat in the growing dark, lights shining through the windows and smoke curling out of most of the chimneys. The sun had set by the time Ah-Kee and me rode up the muddy main street into town, but only barely, and the sky was still lit up by the oranges and purples of its dying light.

It was a bigger town than Wenatchee by far, but no bigger than it had been the last time I'd come through. Less than a year had passed, but it sure enough felt longer. An awful lot had happened since I'd last ridden up that horse-mucked street. Back then I'd been in a wagon with my family. Now I was on a borrowed Indian pony, with a Chinese boy's arms squeezing the life out of me. He'd stayed on the horse, though, by God, and the pony's feet had eaten up the miles.

I was wasting no time. There were several hotels and bars and stables, and I was betting that somewhere among them I'd find Ezra Bishop and with him, my horse at last.

I started asking folks that we passed, but either folks didn't know Mr. Bishop or they weren't willing to tell where he was. Some folks just shot a dirty look at Ah-Kee and kept walking without even answering.

All of a sudden I heard Ah-Kee gasp. His arms let go of me and he dropped down to the ground, but on purpose for once. He held up a finger to me, spoke a few urgent words, then scurried into a nearby store, still open and well-lit with oil lamps.

My heart sank when I saw the sign for it. A Chinese laundry. Through the window I could see the Chinese man standing behind the crude counter. The door closed behind Ah-Kee.

He'd found his own people.

I'd known it would happen—heck, it was why I'd brought him along in the first place. But, truth be told, I'd gotten to like having Ah-Kee around. I wasn't ready yet to go back to being all alone again. I cursed softly in the darkness.

I was just about to spur the horse forward when I took one last look at Ah-Kee through the laundry window. He was talking to the man across the counter. He held something up, and I squinted to see it through the dirty glass. It was that bird sculpture again. The man answered back, shaking his head and shrugging his shoulders.

To my surprise, Ah-Kee turned and walked back out to me.

His face showed his disappointment. He held up his hand so I could help him back up onto the horse.

"You coming with me?" I asked, sounding a bit happier than I intended. "You ain't staying here, with your own people?"

He just kept his hand up, waiting. His whole body spoke of sadness, standing there in the mud looking up at me.

"I have no idea what you're looking for, Ah-Kee," I said as I reached down and lifted him up behind me. "But I sure hope you find it."

A few buildings farther up the street was a kind of trading post and general store, dark and closed. A man was just latching the front door when we came up.

"Excuse me, sir," I said. "I'm looking for a man and I was wondering if you knew where he was."

The man looked us up and down. He was bundled up against the evening chill and seemed in a hurry to get home or to whatever saloon he was heading for.

"What's his name?"

"Ezra Bishop, sir. He's a horse trader, of sorts."

The man's face soured into a scowl.

"Sure, I know Ezra Bishop. He was here this afternoon trying to cheat me on a load of furs. He's gone now, though."

My head dropped and I almost swore out loud. I was sure making a regular habit of ending up where Ezra Bishop had just been. My body and mind were tired of this cross-country chasing, but my heart still pulled me along like a sled dog toward my pony.

"Oh," I said. "Thank you, sir. I don't suppose you know which way he was headed?"

The man pointed up the street, toward the fading light of the sun.

"Thataway."

"West? Over the mountains to Seattle?" My heart did a double-drop. I had sworn I'd get Sarah back or die trying, and the second option was looking more and more likely if I was gonna have to head over the Cascade Mountains in October on foot.

"Seattle? No, boy. Just right up there to the Robber's Roost Saloon, three doors up. He's stabling his horses there and staying in the little house out back. Still there, as far as I know."

My head snapped up and my heart set to racing. Sarah was three doors up the street. If I shouted she'd likely hear me. After three days of mountain passes and grizzly bears and Indian races, I was a stone's throw away from my horse at last.

"Thank you, sir," I said quick, spurring the horse on. "Much obliged."

The horse couldn't go fast enough up that road to make my heart happy. Ellensburg was a busy town, even at dusk, and we had to weave between men on horseback and wagons and people afoot. Then there it was, oil lamps burning in the windows and a rough hand-lettered sign above the door: THE ROBBER'S ROOST SALOON.

As we rode up I craned my neck to see behind it, and sure enough there was a stable there, closed up for the night, and a shabby little cabin beside it. Smoke was coming from the cabin's chimney, and through the one window I saw the shadow of a large man move in front of the fire.

Ezra Bishop, the man I'd been seeking, was in that cabin.

And in that stable, just waiting for me to find her and hug her and have her back, was my Sarah.

My hands were shaking with excitement, and I sure enough wanted nothing more in the world than to just go straight back there and find her. I figured I could have her out of there in under a minute and be off in the darkness, back where I belonged with the horse that belonged with me.

But I knew I couldn't do that. I was no horse thief. Papa would never have allowed it. And besides, horse thieves weren't looked upon kindly by anybody. If I was caught it sure wouldn't have been good. I didn't think they'd hang a twelve-year-old boy, but they'd be tempted. And I'd likely lose any chance I had of getting Sarah back.

Ezra Bishop had bought and paid for her, and I s'posed it weren't his fault that the seller had no right to her. I'd have to get her back honest or not at all.

I steered the pony through the gap between the Robber's Roost and its neighbor, around to the back. Through the stable walls I heard the snort of a horse, and I almost cried out. Could that be my Sarah, only inches away? I forced myself to calm down and think things through. It was a dicey situation for sure.

I sat for a second on the pony, considering it all.

"All right, let's get down," I whispered to Ah-Kee over my shoulder. "But be quiet about it." I felt Ah-Kee's head nod against my back, and we slid on down to the ground with as little noise as we could. Ah-Kee looked at me with big, questioning eyes. I wished I could explain it all to him. He didn't even know we was after a horse at all, let alone a horse owned by a bad man who wasn't likely to want to sell her to me for less than he paid for her.

The cabin was small and dark, with a little covered porch out front. Quiet as I could, I led Ah-Kee around to the side, among some scattered tools where the shadows were thickest.

"Stay here," I said, motioning as clear as I could for him to crouch down and stay put. I didn't know how Mr. Bishop felt about Chinese folks, but so far most white folks around here didn't seem to like them. I didn't want having Ah-Kee there with me to spoil the deal, and I didn't want Ah-Kee in any danger, neither. "I'll be back out here quick as I can, and then you and me'll ride off together on the finest horse you ever saw." I knew Ah-Kee didn't know a darn word of what I was saying—I was saying it more for myself than for him. The truth was, I was scared so bad I felt like I was gonna lose whatever little food I had left in my belly.

I could tell Ah-Kee didn't like me leaving him there alone, though whether he was more worried about himself or me, I couldn't tell. We'd already been through plenty together, Ah-Kee and me, and I felt awful alone as I walked around the corner of that cabin and up onto the front porch.

I stood for a second looking at the crooked plank door. Through it I could hear someone big walking around inside. Even in that chilly evening air my palms and underarms were sweating like summertime.

I heard Papa's voice in my head. *If there's something that's got to be done, then the thing to do is just to buckle down and do it as best you can.*

Mama piped in, too. *"If you got a brave spirit and a true heart, Joseph, you can hold your head up and take on any trouble."* I didn't know how brave my spirit was, but my heart was sure enough beating true for the horse my papa had bought for me and my mama had named for me. She was mine and I was there to get her, by God.

I reached up with the bravest spirit I could muster and knocked three times firm on the door.

There was a creaking of floorboards and then the door was jerked open roughly. It was dark inside and the huge, hulking shadow was backlit by a fire in the stone fireplace. I thought I recognized the burly shoulders, though, and the bushy black beard that stood out on the man's face and hung all the way down to the second button on his shirt.

"Ezra Bishop?" I asked, just to be sure.

"Who the hell is asking?" a voice barked, drunk and already angry.

CHAPTER
10

The shadow swayed slightly from side to side before me. Even from outside I could smell the familiar perfume of whiskey and someone who'd been drinking too much of it. I knew that stink well from my cursed days with Mr. Grissom.

"My name's Joseph Johnson, sir. I believe you have something that belongs to me."

"You *what*? Something that belongs to *you*? What are you saying, boy?"

I realized my mistake immediately. I'd just knocked on his door and accused him of horse-thieving.

"No, sir," I rushed to say. "I meant to say you have something that I would like to buy. A horse, sir. You bought her, and I've come to buy her back."

The shadow stepped forward into the doorway, and I looked up into the face of Ezra Bishop. I'd had those black beady eyes and pockmarked face in my mind's eye since the moment I'd found my Sarah missing. He was even larger than I remembered, a bulging giant of a man who filled the whole of the door frame. He was big as a bull, with a broad barrel chest, but he had the softness around his face and belly of a man who was too fond of his bottle and his bacon.

He smacked his lips and rocked back on his heels. "You got money, boy?"

"Yes, sir," I said. I patted the satchel around my shoulder. "I've come prepared to pay you, fair and honest."

In an instant I saw the man before me change. His eyes cleared, his jaw tightened. The lazy looseness of his body disappeared.

Before we'd left Missouri to come west, our neighbors'd had a dog. He was a friendly dog, all wagging tail and flopping tongue. But that was only with people. With other dogs he was truly a terror—he fought red-hot and without warning, and had killed more than one dog unfortunate enough to wander into his sight. I remembered petting him once, when he was lying about in the dust on a sunny day, panting happily. Then he saw another dog down the road a ways. His eyes had sharpened, and his shoulders bunched; the fur rose quiet and angry up his back, his tongue disappeared, and his teeth showed white. His whole body had gone still and ready, like the hammer on a pistol poised to fire. He'd been ready for blood.

Mr. Bishop had done just the same thing. At the mere mention of money, he'd sobered right up. And I knew he was ready to show his teeth.

"Come in, then," he said, turning around and sauntering into the cabin. "Let's talk business."

I risked a glance to the corner of the porch, where I saw Ah-Kee's face peeking 'round the corner. I nodded at him real quick and then screwed up my courage and stepped inside the cabin. I left the door standing open behind me, though. I reckoned when you walk into a bear's cave, keeping an eye on the exit ain't never a bad idea.

It was a filthy mess on the inside, with gear and clothes thrown everywhere around the one room. Apple cores and empty bottles littered the dirty plank floor. Based on the smell hitting my nose, I'd have wagered there was a chamber pot or two somewhere in the shadows as well. It was a nastier hive than Mr. Grissom's place, which I hadn't thought was possible, and it was hot and stuffy from the blazing fire. I started sweating all over again.

Ezra Bishop sat down with a grunt in a chair that creaked under his weight. He waved a hand at a stool sitting nearby. "Take a seat."

"No, thank you, sir. I'd rather stand." Something about the man made me want to stay out of grabbing range of him.

"Suit yourself." He uncorked a bottle with a hollow *plonk* and held it out to me. "I always like to drink while making a deal. Help yourself." I stared at the bottle. Firelight flickered off its grimy surface and the brown liquid sloshing inside.

No one had ever offered me whiskey before. I hated being thought of as a child, but I sure wasn't flattered. I suddenly felt trapped in that little cabin. I was hot and scared and ready to be done with it and there wasn't one bone in my body that liked or trusted the man in front of me. I'm afraid that showed in my voice when I spoke next.

"No, sir. I'd just like to get right to the business at hand."

His eyes narrowed into a squint.

"What wrong I done you, boy? Why you comin' after me lookin' for trouble?"

His voice was a low growl, seething and sharp and soft. He rose to his feet, towering over me.

"You look familiar," he said suspiciously. "Are you from those Injuns I got the better of up on Colockum?"

"No, sir."

"Oh, hell, you from them Entiat folks? You still sore about that horse deal?"

"No, sir," I answered, wondering just how many enemies Ezra Bishop had made on this trip.

"Oh, wait," he said, pointing at me with a blunt finger. "I know you. Up at Mission! The orphan kid."

"I ain't an orphan."

"I bought your horse, right? That stubborn little Injun one?"

I swallowed hard to keep my anger where it needed to be, in my belly. A fight with Ezra Bishop was one I could not win, and I sure enough knew it.

"Yes, sir. You had no way of knowing it, sir, but Mr. Grissom had no right to sell that horse. She's mine, and I've come to buy her back."

"God, that filly is a vicious nag! I had to whip her up one side of the mountain and down the other."

I ground my teeth so hard I was afraid they was gonna shatter.

"Well, then," I said, clenching my fists to keep my voice even, "I reckon you'll be happy to get her off your hands, sir."

Ezra Bishop took a wet slurp out of the bottle. It looked

like more of an act than real drinking. Like he was playing a part. I swallowed nervously. The man before me didn't seem sloppy anymore, but cold and shrewd. And dangerous.

"She was a hard one to handle, that one," he said, his eyes sharp as railroad spikes.

"Was, sir?"

His eyes darted to the satchel over my shoulder.

"You say you brought money for her? How much you bring, boy?"

I licked my lips. This was the part I'd been dreading since leaving the trading post in Wenatchee.

"Well, sir, I've got sixty-two dollars and fifty cents, ready to hand over to you to get my property."

"She became *my* property when I bought and paid for her, boy. And I paid *eighty* dollars, square." His voice was tight and tense. It sounded as dangerous to me as the cold, deadly buzz of a rattlesnake. This was a man who lived by making dirty deals. I had no idea how I was gonna out-bargain Mr. Ezra Bishop.

"Yes, sir, I know. But I have incurred some expenses in my efforts to catch you." I tried squeezing in every fancy word I knew, in hopes of dazzling him into agreement. Maybe all them newspapers my mama'd made me read were gonna pay off.

"Incurred some expenses?"

"Yes, sir. Provisions and such. And besides, you won two races with my horse up at the racing grounds. A pile of furs and some horses, I hear. So you've made your profit on my horse already, way I see it."

"The way *you* see it? Way I see it is this: She. Ain't. Your. Horse. And you're forty dollars short."

"Forty? But you only paid eighty and—"

"And I whipped and dragged that horse forty miles. You gotta pay me for time and trouble, boy. A dollar a mile."

I felt my heart start to break, but I knew I had to be some kind of strong. It's what Papa would expect, and what my Sarah needed.

"I don't got forty more dollars, sir. But maybe we could work something out; maybe I could work it off in labor, or—"

"How'd you catch up to me so fast?"

"Sir?"

"I've been riding fast, getting here. How'd you get here so quick, only one day behind me?"

"On foot, mostly. But the Indians lent me a horse up on Colockum, so I made quick time today."

Mr. Bishop's eyebrows rose.

"You got an Indian horse? You never said *that*. That horse and your sixty-two and change would be just about right."

"I can't give you that horse, sir. She ain't mine to give."

"Get your money out, boy. Let me see it."

He took a step toward me. I didn't like nothing about what I heard in his voice. I remembered what Frank Jameson had warned me: *You keep your wits about you, and don't give him a red cent 'til he hands you the bridle to that pony of yours.*

"Let me see my horse, sir."

"She ain't your damned horse!" he shouted. He took another step toward me. "Give me the money, and I'll trade you a horse for that Indian pony you rode in on."

Warnings went off in my mind like Fourth of July fireworks. Ezra Bishop's words weren't adding up in my mind.

"I don't want a horse, sir. I want *my* horse. And I want to see her now."

He took two more steps forward, kicking over the stool he'd offered me.

I backed up quick, toward the door.

"You don't have her, do you? You don't have my horse."

"*Damn* it, boy, she ain't your horse!"

I looked him right in his devilish eyes and there was sure enough steel in my voice when I spoke.

"Yes, she is. She'll always be my horse, no matter what."

"We made a deal." His voice was like a cougar's hiss now, hungry and hateful. Another step toward me, another step of my own toward the door behind me. "Give me that money and I'll give you a horse."

"We made no deal, Mr. Bishop. Tell me where my horse is."

He was too close for me to go for my gun; by the time I had it out of my satchel he'd be on me, and I was no match for his brawn. He'd have me, my money, and Papa's gun before I could get my finger on the trigger.

I was standing there, thinking like a fever about all my bad options, when Ezra Bishop snarled and thundered toward me. I backpedaled quick out the doorway and into the gathering darkness of the night, stumbling off the porch and falling flat on my back in the dirt. He followed after, squinting at me from the doorway.

That's when I saw Ah-Kee, standing up against the front of the cabin, just to the side of the door. He had a shovel gripped in his hands, and that shovel's head glinted in the blue light of the moon that had risen in the night sky. His eyes were on Ezra Bishop, and his body tensed, ready to strike.

"No!" I shouted. "Don't!"

But at that moment, Ezra Bishop squared himself in the cabin doorway.

"I will!" he roared. "We have a deal!"

He took a ragged step out the door, into the moonlight.

With a grunt Ah-Kee swung the shovel. It sliced through the air and the flat side of it caught Ezra Bishop flat in the face with a sickening *thwock* that echoed and died in the night air behind the Robber's Roost.

Ezra Bishop crumpled to the ground like a sack of rotten onions.

I looked, gasping, to Ah-Kee's stunned face, the shovel still in his hands, then to the limp body of Mr. Bishop.

"Deal's off," I whispered in the moonlight.

CHAPTER
11

From the street behind me, on the other side of the Robber's Roost Saloon, I heard laughter and the muffled sound of people talking.

No shouts of alarm. No running footsteps.

I waited a moment more, breathless.

Ezra Bishop didn't move, lying facedown in the dirt. Neither did I, frozen there on the ground with my heart pounding. Neither did Ah-Kee, still holding the shovel that had brought Ezra Bishop down.

We three were like a picture from a dime novel, struck still in the moonlight. But this weren't no novel.

"Ah-Kee," I said. "This is bad."

He lowered the shovel. I could hear his lungs working from where I stood.

I stood up and stepped toward Ezra Bishop's body, bracing my soul for the worst. But then I saw his back rise and fall.

"Thank the Lord," I breathed. "He's alive. But he sure won't be happy when he comes to."

I stood looking down at the sleeping giant.

"Ah-Kee, when he wakes up he's gonna be looking for blood! And you being Chinese, well, shoot—I reckon no one'd think twice before stringing you up from the nearest . . ." I stopped my panicked yammering when I saw Ah-Kee still standing there, his face a mask of fear. My words were a mess to him, but I'm sure he could tell that I was terrified and unhappy. I thought about what he'd done. He'd heard the shouting and he'd left his hiding place and crept out with that shovel. Coming to help *me*. He'd risked his neck and at the very least saved my money and my only shot at getting Sarah back. Heck, he may have even saved my life. Who knew what a man like Mr. Bishop was capable of?

I walked over to him and gently took the shovel from his hands and set it down. Then I held my hand out to him. He looked at it for a second, then understood and reached out to shake it.

"Thank you, Ah-Kee," I said. His face and shoulders relaxed just a bit. "That was awful brave. Not as brave as talking down a grizzly, maybe." I looked back down at Mr. Bishop, who grunted and jerked and then went back still. "But it's right up there."

A few buildings down, a door creaked open. Someone stepped outside; my breath stopped. There was some grumbling and a clatter of glass, then the door closed and the alley got quiet again. From the street I heard some shouting, and the sounds of a wagon passing by.

"All right, Ah-Kee, we gotta get him inside fast before someone sees him. Grab a foot."

Ezra Bishop was the heaviest thing I'd ever had to try and move. Picking him up, even with the two of us, was out of the question. Even dragging him was a trial. We each grabbed hold of one of his monstrous feet and had to put all our bodies into it to inch him back up onto the porch and into the doorway. His arms dragged behind him, hanging above his head like he was at gunpoint. When his shoulders hit the door frame he stopped solid and Ah-Kee went stumbling forward without him, ending up tangled in a pile of ropes.

I stood, panting for breath, while Ah-Kee got himself untangled and stood up.

He stood there a second, then started cursing and swearing in Chinese, his voice all choked and high.

"What's the matter, Ah-Kee?" I hissed, trying to quiet him down. He held something out to me in the firelight. It was Ezra Bishop's boot. "All right, so what's the—" That's when the smell hit me, stopping my words with a gag.

"Good God Almighty!" I coughed, covering my nose with my arm. "That's the worst thing I ever smelled, and Mr. Grissom used to make me clean the privy!" Ah-Kee was still swearing up a blue streak in Chinese, his nose wrinkled and his eyes screwed shut. "Put it back on, Ah-Kee! Get that thing back on his foot!" I waved my arm frantically toward Ezra Bishop's exposed stocking foot. A big, hairy toe stuck out a hole.

Ah-Kee got the boot back on with plenty of swearing and gagging and we dragged him the rest of the way in and got the door shut behind us. Mr. Bishop was starting to rock and moan a bit, and I knew we needed to figure our next move out quick.

The pile of ropes that Ah-Kee had fallen into caught my eye. I looked around and saw the sturdy post in the middle of the room that held up the crossbeam of the roof. Papa had taught me plenty before he died, and one of the things he taught me best was tying knots. *"A man's gotta know ropes, and a man's gotta know knots,"* is what he said, and I was sure enough thankful for it right then.

Quick as we could, we rolled him over to the post and got him sitting up against it. He was moaning steady by then and his head was kinda lolling from side to side on his wobbly neck. Time was running out and I worked fast. In no time, using Papa's knots, I had Ezra Bishop's arms bound tight as a barrel behind him, 'round the post. For good measure I tied a rope 'round his waist, too, and bound his stinking feet together to keep his wiggling and kicking to a minimum.

I was confident in the ropes and in the knots Papa'd taught me. Ezra Bishop weren't going nowhere.

I knew he was gonna wake up any minute but there was something I had to check. "Wait here," I told Ah-Kee, then ran to the door. He looked more than a little displeased to be left alone with Ezra Bishop, even with him being tied up, but I dashed outside, promising to be quick.

I ran right up to the stable and swung open the door, and my fears were confirmed.

There were only two horses stabled there. A big sturdy bay that I recognized as Mr. Bishop's from his visit to Mr. Grissom's. And an old bent-back gray mare that I could tell even in the darkness didn't have too many miles left in her.

I reckoned sure enough that was the horse Ezra Bishop would have given me if I'd have made the deal. Dirty swindler.

When I got back into the cabin Ezra Bishop was still out cold. Ah-Kee was standing warily across the room, as far as he could from our prisoner. I saw that he'd fetched the shovel from the porch and held it tightly in both hands, ready for another swing.

"Good thinking," I said with a smile, closing the door behind me. My thoughts were racing fast. When Ezra Bishop came to he was gonna be madder than a wet nest of hornets, but I badly needed some information from him. "What does Ezra Bishop care about most?" I asked myself out loud, and it didn't take long for me to come up with an answer. I dug quickly through the piled-up mess around the cabin, desperately seeking the one thing I knew Ezra Bishop would do anything for.

In a big leather folding case, inside a saddlebag under the bed, I found it.

Ezra Bishop's money. I flipped through it. He'd had a good trip of horse buying and selling, Mr. Bishop had. I counted more than six hundred dollars, in everything from one dollar bills up to a couple of crisp hundreds.

I dragged the stool right over by the fire and sat on it, facing Mr. Bishop, the leather money case at my feet. From my own satchel I pulled out Papa's pistol and set it across my knees and waited. Ah-Kee pulled the other chair over and sat next to me, the shovel resting on his shoulder. We were quite a pair, Ah-Kee and I. We looked in silence at our captive with his greasy black beard and bulging stomach and the beginnings of a shovel-shaped bruise starting to darken across his forehead. We sat there, waiting for the monster to wake up.

And then he did.

And it weren't slow, like I was expecting.

All of a sudden he jerked and his legs kicked and his eyes shot wide open.

He blinked at us, breathing fast through his nose, confusion all over his face.

"What the hell's going on?" he asked in a yell, then winced. "God, my head!" he said quieter.

"I'm gonna make this fast, sir. We ain't gonna do you any more harm unless you give us a reason to. I just need you to tell me where my horse is."

"Why the hell would I tell you anything?" he growled, still wincing with one eye and keeping his voice low.

"Because I'm asking you nicely, sir, and you've got no reason to not answer. Just tell me where my horse is, and we'll be on our way."

"You gotta funny way of being nice, boy. I'm tied and bound with a headache that'd kill a buffalo. Why shouldn't I just start yelling bloody murder and get help a-coming?"

I picked the pistol up off my knee and rested it, real casual-like, across my arm so that its unblinking barrel was pointed vaguely but without question in the direction of Ezra Bishop's stinking body.

"Here's one reason, sir."

"Bull. You ain't never gonna—"

"I know how this is s'posed to go, sir," I cut in. "This is where you tell me that I ain't never gonna shoot you. That I'm just a boy and all that. I've had this conversation before. The last fella was wrong, and you are, too." Mr. Bishop's eyes widened, and I swallowed nervously. I was playing a bit of a bluff here, and I had to play it well. "You are a liar and a thief, sir. You took my horse and you cheated those Indians and you were gonna take my money. I don't think most folks would find too much fault if a fella like you ended up with a bullet in him. And I don't think they'd cast too much blame if it were just a boy like me, defending myself against a violent swindler like you, who sent that bullet on its way." I lowered my voice and fixed Mr. Bishop with what I hoped was a murderous, cold-hearted stare. "If I were you, I sure enough wouldn't doubt me like Mr. Grissom did when I found out he'd sold you my horse." The way I said it sure made it sound like I'd shot Mr. Grissom, and I was gonna let that illusion lie where it was. Ezra Bishop thinking that I'd already killed a man was a point in my favor that I wasn't giving away.

Ezra Bishop's eyes narrowed and slid over to Ah-Kee and his shovel.

"Who the hell is he?"

"That there is Ah-Kee. I wouldn't trifle with him, neither. Your forehead can already testify as to his strength and skill with that shovel." I stuck my foot out, showing the shredded pants and dried blood from the grizzly's claws. "This here is from a mama grizzly we come across up Colockum. She was getting the better of me before Ah-Kee stepped in. She ain't bothering nobody no more. Ah-Kee here knows some dark arts of the Orient that you don't wanna get on the wrong side of."

Mr. Bishop looked pale in the firelight. His eyes darted from Ah-Kee to my bloody leg.

"Mama grizzly, you say?"

"That's right. Now, where did my horse go?"

Ezra Bishop cleared his throat and looked quick from Ah-Kee to me.

"Well, boy, I ain't sure I can quite exactly recall. That was quite a hit to the head I took. Maybe a little bit of green would clear my head some." He was not the kind of man who was used to getting the bad end of a deal, and I reckoned even tied up at gunpoint facing two savage killer boys he weren't gonna give up so easy on coming out ahead.

"True," I answered after a moment, looking him right in the eye. "Maybe a little bit of money *would* help the situation." Ezra Bishop smiled a small greedy smile and licked his lips, but his smile went running right away when I pulled his own leather money bag up onto my lap.

"That's mine!" he shouted, then grimaced in pain and spoke again, quieter. "That's mine. You can't take my money."

"No, sir. My mama didn't raise no thief, that's for sure. I ain't leaving here with a nickel of your money." I pulled a rumpled five dollar note from the case and held it casually in my hand, kind of over toward the fire. "But I'm clumsy, see. And you never know if I'm gonna drop some of your hard-stolen money too close to that fire."

"You wouldn't."

I flicked my wrist and let the money slip from my fingers. We all watched it flutter toward the flames and come to rest just shy of the glowing coals at the fire's edge. The corners of the bill folded and blackened and a dark burn spread slowly across it.

"You little wretch," Ezra Bishop seethed.

"What did you do with my horse, Mr. Bishop?"

"You and your dirty little friend, coming into my—"

Mr. Bishop stopped talking when another bill, this time a one dollar note, flew right into the center of the fire and commenced to turning directly into ashes.

"That's for being rude to Ah-Kee. There's only one devil in this room and he is, thank the Lord, tied up to a post." I pulled a ten dollar bill from the case and held it up. "When are you gonna start talking, Mr. Bishop?"

Ezra Bishop chewed on his cheeks so hard I expected to see blood coming down his chin any second. His eyes were twice as fierce and angry as the grizzly's had been. I said a silent prayer that my knots were true, or else I knew I'd sure enough end up using Papa's pistol after all.

"I sold her," Ezra Bishop finally said through gritted teeth.

"When?"

"This afternoon."

"Who'd you sell her to?"

"A man."

"I figured he was a man. I need a name, Mr. Bishop." I held the ten dollar bill a little closer to the fire.

"John Campbell! His name's John Campbell!"

"Good. Where's he live?"

"Hell if I know."

I balled up the bill in my hand and raised my arm to throw it.

"No! I don't know where he lives! He's a horse trader like me, moving around! I sold him my whole string!"

I ground my teeth. It figured. More moving, more chasing, more never quite finding my horse.

"All right, sir. And where is this John Campbell heading with my horse?"

"Come on, boy, I can't go sending a couple of wild animals after the man. I got a reputation to think about."

"Your reputation is in worse shape than your socks, Mr. Bishop. You best be worried more about your money at the moment." The ten dollar bill flew into the fire like a doomed bird. Ezra Bishop made a groan like a physical pain.

"Okay, okay, by God! No more! He's heading to Walla Walla, through Yakima. He aims to sell your pony and the rest to a man by the name of Carl Rasmussen. Rasmussen has a regular business sending western horses and Indian ponies on the train back east. They fetch top dollar out there. Campbell's s'posed to meet up with Rasmussen in Walla Walla in seven day's time."

My heart beat cold as a winter wind. My sweet Sarah, crowded up in a boxcar and shipped a thousand miles away? The thought was too much to bear.

I stood up and let the rest of Mr. Bishop's money fall to the floor at my feet. He looked up at me, eyes wide and angry.

I grabbed a rag off the floor and walked around behind him.

"Now, we can't have you hollering as soon as we walk out that door. Open your mouth, sir."

"You gonna gag me with that, boy? Why, you mean, low-down little—"

"No, sir. If I was mean and low-down I'd use your sock."

"But I gotta use the privy and—"

"Well, I apologize for that," I answered, jamming the cloth between his teeth, "but I reckon you got enough money left to buy yourself a new pair of pants." I started to tie it behind his head, but Ah-Kee stopped me with an insistent word.

He rose to his feet and walked slowly to stand before Mr. Bishop, the shovel still held in his hands.

Ezra Bishop spit out the rag.

"What's he doing?" he croaked. I didn't answer, 'cause I didn't know.

Ah-Kee knelt down on the floor by Mr. Bishop, looking solemnly into his eyes. Mr. Bishop flinched when Ah-Kee moved the shovel, but he only rested it gently across our prisoner's legs. Then he pulled that little black bird out of his pocket once more. And again, as I'd seen him do four other times, he held it out to Mr. Bishop and said a soft string of words. And again it ended with a clear but mysterious question.

"Oh, God, what's he saying?" Mr. Bishop muttered to me under his breath.

I sure enough didn't know. I'd have given just about anything to find out what my friend was seeking. He was on a mission of his own, that much was clear. And it was a mission that he was willing to kneel at the foot of the devil for. But it was as mysterious to me as the words he spoke.

When Mr. Bishop didn't answer him, Ah-Kee returned the stone bird to his pocket, reclaimed the shovel, and rose to stand a few steps away.

I stuffed the rag back in Mr. Bishop's mouth and tied it tight behind his head. I moved around in front of him.

Ezra Bishop mumbled something through his gag that didn't sound too friendly. I hunkered down on my heels so I could look him right in his eyes.

"I know you're plenty angry, sir. But I'm leaving you unharmed and without a dime of your money in my pockets. I sure reckon you wouldn't have done me the same favor if our parts had been reversed." He blinked at me sulkily.

"The fire'll keep you warm for the night, and we'll send someone for you before we leave town. I would count yourself lucky and not make the mistake of coming after us. It won't end as well for you the second time around, I promise you that. I kept Ah-Kee under control this time, but he's one rattlesnake you can't keep caged for long. My heart shudders to think what that boy would do to you if he sees you again."

Ezra Bishop looked over at Ah-Kee and his shovel. A beady shine of sweat popped out on his forehead. Ah-Kee looked at us uncertainly; he could tell we were talking about him. He flashed us a small, unsure smile that in the firelight might just have looked like a mountain lion's snarl, if you were afraid enough.

"God," I whispered to Ezra Bishop. "That cold heart of his is as black as coal. He's smiling just thinking about it." I felt the big man shiver. "You best keep your distance, sir," I breathed in his ear, patting him on the shoulder.

"Come on, Ah-Kee," I said, standing up. "Time to go."

Ah-Kee dropped the shovel to the floor with a loud crash. Ezra Bishop's whole body jumped and flinched and he brought his bound feet up to his chest.

Outside, in the moonlight, the Indian pony was waiting for us. She'd wandered over by the door, no doubt wondering where her people were. I looked around at the little porch, and my eye stuck on something: a whip, dark and thin, coiled up like a snake on a barrel top. It was Mr. Bishop's whip—the very one he'd beaten my Sarah with, no doubt. Who knows how many terrified horses that devil had whipped with it? I picked it up and wrapped it around my shoulder.

Ah-Kee looked at me, and I shrugged.

"Sometimes taking something from someone is exactly what the Lord would want you to do," I said, and I figured Mama and Papa would have agreed.

I sighed, tired to my very bones. All this time I'd thought all I had to do was catch up to Ezra Bishop. But now, after all I'd been through, it turned out that the crooked horse dealer was not the end of my road. I had more miles to go, more men to find.

But I knew there was no stopping now. My goal all along had not been to find Ezra Bishop. It was to rescue my Sarah. And I knew I'd go to hell itself if I had to to get her back.

"Let's go," I said, patting Ah-Kee on his shoulder and stepping out toward the pony. "We gotta beat a horse to Walla Walla."

CHAPTER
12

We were back on Ellensburg's main road and my mind was halfway to Walla Walla when I remembered that the horse we were riding wasn't ours. I swore out loud and brought her to a halt. It would have been the easiest thing in the world to just keep on going right outta town with that strong little pony. They'd never have found me, and no one would have ever been the wiser. But Mr. Strawn's words echoed in my head: *These folks have had enough taken from them.*

"Excuse me, sir?" I asked a man walking up the road. "Could you tell me where the Indian agent's office is?"

"Indian agent?" the man asked. He wore the sturdy boots and floppy hat of a miner, and the blurry smile of a drunk. "Looks like you need to find yerself the Chinese agent!" He pointed up at Ah-Kee and fell into a fit of laughter.

I bit my tongue to keep my frustration from coming out as angry words.

"Yes, sir. But do you know where the Indian agent is?"

The man burped and scratched at his belly.

" 'Course I do. You're talking about Jed Holcomb. You're heading the right way, even. Jes' head on down to the next block, take a right, and it's the last building on your way outta town."

"Thank you, sir."

The Indian agent's office was its own little tidy wooden building on the very edge of Ellensburg, with a corral and stable out back. It all looked fairly dark and empty but I knocked on the door anyhow, and there was some rustling inside and then the door swung open, revealing a man with a black handlebar mustache. He was wearing a red union suit that stretched from his neck to his ankles, and held a sputtering oil lamp in his hand.

"I'm sorry to bother you, sir. My name is Joseph Johnson. You are Jed Holcomb, sir, the Indian agent?"

"Last time I checked. Whatcha need, son? I was just crawling in."

"I've got a pony that I'm to leave with you. It's from Chief George. He lent me its use to get down the Colockum, and he'll pick it up here in a couple days."

"Chief George let you have one of his horses?"

"He let us borrow one, sir. If you're indisposed, I can stable her myself and then be on my way."

Jed Holcomb cocked his head at me and scratched at his mustache. "Why in the world did ol' George let you borrow one of his horses? He's a good man and a friend of mine, but I've never known him to be sending his horses off with strangers, and a child no less."

"It's a long story, sir."

The man stepped back and beckoned me inside.

"Well come in and tell it, then. It's gotta be a good one."

"I ain't alone, sir," I said, staying right where I was. I'd had about enough of folks being rude to Ah-Kee. "I'll just leave the pony and be on my way."

The man peered past me and saw Ah-Kee standing by the pony. His face didn't lose its friendly expression.

"Well, heck, he's smaller than you are! You think I don't got room for the both of you? Just get the pony in the corral for now and come on in the back, the pair of you."

A few minutes later Ah-Kee and I sat on sawed-off logs by the fire, chewing on cold potato stew the man had left over from dinner. The gristly meat that required five chews to get down was a mystery better left unsolved, but the meal was met with much rejoicing by my empty belly.

"We sure do appreciate this, sir," I said between mouthfuls. "It's been a number of days since either one of us had a decent meal."

"You're more than welcome. Now, tell me how it is you ended up with a pony from Chief George."

I told him the whole business, starting with Mr. Grissom back in Mission. I left out the bits about my pants falling down and all of Ah-Kee's tumbles from the horse, and truth be told I s'pose it did make a pretty good yarn. When I got to our encounter with Ezra Bishop, I skipped over the shovel and the gun and the tying and gagging. I just told him that we'd learned that Mr. Bishop had sold my pony to Mr. Campbell, who was now on his way to Yakima and then Walla Walla.

Jed Holcomb let out a low whistle when I was through.

"You boys done had a time of it," he said. He looked at me serious for a moment, firelight shining in his eyes. "That horse means a lot to you, don't she?"

I fought the lump in my throat.

"More than anything in the world, sir. She's all I got."

"I understand, son. What's more, John Campbell will, too. He's a good man. He deals straight and treats the Indians fair. If you tell him what you told me, he'll sell you your horse back. We just gotta get you to Yakima before Campbell leaves. And I reckon I know just how to do it. You can head out first thing in the morning."

"In the morning? I was hoping to get a move on tonight."

Mr. Holcomb shook his head.

"No point, son. Mr. Campbell is well away, and on foot in this dark you won't gain any ground. I got something else in mind that should have you in Yakima a heckuva lot quicker, and with a night's rest and a breakfast in you."

He stood up and took our now-empty bowls.

"There's only the one bed in here, but you boys can sleep in the stable. There's fresh hay that's a fair piece softer than my old mattress, and I got plenty of blankets to keep you warm."

I wanted to argue, wanted to keep pushing after my Sarah, who was now so close I could feel her heart calling to me. But just hearing the words *sleep* and *blanket* were about enough to melt my tired bones into a puddle. And my belly didn't mind hearing the word *breakfast*, neither.

"Thank you, sir. That'd be much appreciated."

Mr. Holcomb gestured to Ah-Kee, sitting silent on his log chair.

"He ever talk?"

"Just to grizzlies, sir."

Mr. Holcomb smiled.

"Right. Well, let's turn in. You boys gotta heckuva adventure in store for you tomorrow."

When morning came the next day, it came early and it came cold. Neither Ah-Kee nor myself felt much like getting up when Mr. Holcomb shook us, but I reckon we both knew it was time. The sun was just glowing over the eastward edge of the mountains when we hit the road with a cold breakfast in our bellies. Jed Holcomb and Ah-Kee and I were walking out of Ellensburg, but not on the road to Yakima that climbed up over the hills. We'd just passed the edge of the town, walking on a two-rut wagon road through a grassy pasture. Our breath puffed out in silver clouds as we walked.

"You'd never catch Campbell on the road," Mr. Holcomb was saying. "It's almost all uphill through rough country. It takes you up and around the Teanaway Mountains, see? But," he went on, "since you boys are traveling light with no gear or horses or such, you can take the direct route. *Through* the mountains. On the river."

"On the river, sir?"

"You betcha. It's a straight shot from Ellensburg to Yakima, right through Yakima Canyon. The river's quick but not too wild. And I just happen to know where you can get a boat."

"All right, sir. Well, I sure—" My words stopped in my throat, and I skidded to a stop right there. Ah-Kee, walking along behind me, bumped into my back with an *oof.*

Mr. Holcomb turned around. "What's the matter, son?"

"That over there," I said, pointing at a lonely little bunch of trees off the road a bit. My voice was kind of weak and shaky and not at all like a grown man's, but I didn't care. "That's a cemetery, ain't it?"

"Why, yes. That's the traveler's cemetery. It's a little one, for homesteaders and such passing through."

I swallowed. Walking through the morning dark, I hadn't recognized where we were. Those days a year before had been such a misery that my memories were all fuzzy and patched together. But I recognized the place sure enough now. For the second time in four days, I found the urgency of my mission derailed by an empty cemetery.

"You go on ahead," I said quiet. "I'll catch up. I got to pay my respects."

"You know a person buried over there, son?"

"Yes, sir." I took a few steps off the road and into the long, waving grass. "I know two."

I found their graves, and they weren't no primitive boards like poor Papa's. They were proper stones, straight and graceful. Engraved, too. Papa'd spent nearly all the money we had left for them.

ADELAIDE JOHNSON, one read. 1860–1889. BELOVED MOTHER AND WIFE.

And next to that one: KATIE ANNE JOHNSON. 1883–1889. PRECIOUS DAUGHTER AND SISTER.

I fell to my knees before them.

My mama, with her story-telling rivers.

And Katie, with her angel-wing snow and campfires in heaven.

I had no words to say to them, as I had for Papa. My sadness here went too deep for that. A flood of memories swelled through me. All the million kindnesses my mama had shown me. The honest, earthy smell of her. The feel of her fingernails, scratching softly at my back. Putting cool washcloths on my feverish forehead. Singing me to sleep in the dark evenings.

And my sweet sister, my darling Katie. With a smile that was like sunshine. I could still hear her little voice, singing her songs. Could feel the tight, whole-hearted way she hugged. Could still hear her calling my name. And those bright blue eyes that sparkled like nothing else. My little Katie, who was never shy to tell me she loved me. Right up to the end.

The typhoid had taken them quick. We'd stopped here, in Ellensburg, hoping to let them rest and get well. But there was no getting well. There was only getting worse. Papa was in fits. I don't think he slept for a week, sitting by their side, caring for them. He wanted me to stay out of the wagon, to stay away from them so I didn't catch it myself. But there was no keeping me away, of course. Not when Katie was calling for me. We'd always shared a bed, and she couldn't get to sleep without me. So I'd lay there beside her wasted, feverish little body and let her pinch at my neck the way she did, the gentle way she did that helped her drift off.

"I love you, my Joseph," she'd say, her voice a scratchy whisper.

"I love you, too, sis," I'd answer, and watch her eyelids flutter as she fell off to sleep. And then one night we said those same words and she drifted off the same way and then she never woke up again. Papa carried her little body out of the wagon in the morning before Mama could see it, carried it out wrapped up in a blanket with tears streaming down his face and I saw her blond ringlet curls tumbling out of the end of the blanket and I was sitting by the fire outside and I screamed and wailed when I saw it was her, my little Katie, still and dead.

My mama died the next night. She was all in a fever that day, sick and senseless, so she never knew her Katie had died. That was a blessing. Sure enough. And then it was just me and Papa. Just me and sad, broken-hearted Papa. And Sarah, of course, the horse we all loved. The horse that Mama had named. The horse that balked at strangers and hated saddles but was gentle as a lamb when Katie was up on her back. The horse she weaved little wildflower garlands for and put around her neck. Just me and Papa and Sarah.

Then it was just me and Sarah.

And then it was just me.

My shoulders shook with sobs, kneeling there with my family.

I heard footsteps behind me and tried to get ahold of myself. I wiped at my eyes and looked back to see Ah-Kee standing there, still as a statue, his lips pursed.

I cleared my throat and sniffled and turned back to the gravestones so he wouldn't see my tears.

"Ah-Kee," I said, my voice all husky and shaky. "This here's my sister, Katie."

Ah-Kee stepped forward and out of the side of my eye I saw him bow, slow and serious.

"And this here, this here . . ." My voice broke off, but when something has to be done the thing to do is just to buckle down and do it the best you can. "And this here is my mama."

"Mama," Ah-Kee said. I think he knew the word. He must've picked it up somewhere. He said it soft, with a kind of understanding, and I think mixed up in it was some of his own sadness, too.

He bowed again, lower this time. "Mama," he said again, then spoke a long bit of Chinese. His words went up and down and fast and slow in the funny way of his language. Somewhere in the middle of it I heard the word *Joseph*. But he weren't talking to me, I knew. He was talking to my mama. I don't know what he said, but it sounded quiet, and kind, and respectful.

I sure enough loved Ah-Kee right then for whatever it was he was saying so nice to my mama. When he was done, he bowed once more and stepped back. I wiped at my nose and stood up beside him and looked at those two gravestones, standing there together.

When my mama and my sister died, I had stopped being a child. Papa had been in a storm of grief, and there weren't no one to take care of me like Mama had. So I'd taken care of myself. And I'd taken care of Sarah. Looking at those graves, I could feel the difference between the boy I'd been and what I was now. But I could feel the sameness, too. I was strong from losing them, maybe, but any goodness in me came from having them. And all that goodness was telling me more than ever that I needed to get our horse back. She weren't just my horse. She was their horse, too. She was the only family I had left. And my family took care of each other.

I bent down and kissed the top of my mama's stone. The rock was rough but warm from the morning sun.

"Good-bye, Mama," I whispered. I ran my fingertips over the square letters Papa'd gotten carved there: BELOVED MOTHER.

I stepped to the side and kissed Katie's stone. It was just as warm as Mama's. My fingers found the two words: PRECIOUS and SISTER.

"Good-bye, Katie. I love you, sis."

Jed Holcomb was waiting for us at the river with a crude old dugout canoe that was longer than the wagon my family had come west in. He'd already dragged its nose into the water and was sitting on it.

I'm sure he saw the redness in my eyes, but he had the decency to not bring it up.

"This here's your ticket to get your horse back."

I walked closer and took a look. It was definitely an Indian canoe, cut and hacked and burned out of one big solid log. Two oars rested in its bottom. I looked at him doubtfully.

"These Indian dugouts don't look like much, but they're sturdier than river rock," he assured me. "She'll get you down the river, no doubt about that."

"But whose is it?" I asked.

"Don't worry about that. This has been sitting down here gathering leaves and rat nests for years."

I reckon he could see the uncertainty in my face, because he stood up and looked me in the eye.

"You're a good boy. But I give you my word, son. It ain't stealing."

I trusted Mr. Holcomb. He seemed to be a good man, the kind of man that Papa would have liked. I pulled the paddles out of the boat and handed one to Ah-Kee.

"So how does this work?" I asked.

"Work? You sit in it and go downstream. You steer with the paddles. Get low and hold on at the rough parts. The river will pretty much take care of the rest. Watch out for logjams, though. Them pile-ups where logs and branches and such all get rammed together. Steer clear of those. If you get tangled up in one, the water pulls you right under and it's all over for you before you can even holler for help."

I got myself in the canoe, sitting up on my knees at the front. Ah-Kee clambered in behind me. He looked more scared than I'd ever seen him—and that included with the grizzly and Ezra Bishop.

"Can you swim?" I asked him. Ah-Kee, of course, just blinked back at me.

"Can you?" Jed Holcomb asked me.

"No, sir."

Mr. Holcomb screwed up his lips.

"Well . . . then stay in the boat, son. Keep its nose pointing downstream, and you'll be all right. It's pretty easy and shallow in most parts, far as I know. You'll be in Yakima with that horse of yours in a few hours."

"Thank you, sir. I owe you an awful lot."

"You don't owe me nothing. I was a boy, once, you know. Had a horse, too. Named him Grant, for the general. Big, red bay he was. Like a brother to me. I would've done anything to get that horse back if he'd been stolen from me. A boy like you needs a good horse. And a good horse needs a boy like you. Go and get her. Good luck."

He started to push us off, when it hit me.

"Wait, sir! Ezra Bishop! You need to set him free!"

"Set him free? What are you talking about?"

Quick as I could, I filled Jed Holcomb in on the condition we'd left Ezra Bishop in.

"So could you go and release him? He ain't got no food or nothing, and he's sure enough tied up tight."

Mr. Holcomb stood and looked at me for a moment, a smile playing on his lips under his big black mustache.

"Son, nothing would make me happier than walking over there to see Ezra Bishop gagged and hog-tied. I swear half my job is cleaning up the messes that man makes with the Indians; he deals 'em crooked and bothers their women and gives their young bucks whiskey. It would be my pleasure to release your prisoner." He scratched his jaw thoughtfully. "But . . . I am planning on meeting a friend for lunch. And I've got that Indian pony to take care of. So I'm afraid I might not make it over there 'til about dinnertime." He winked at me, eyes just a-sparkling like a child up to no good. "But I guess he ain't going nowhere, is he?"

And with that, Jed Holcomb pushed us off. The canoe rocked frightfully but stayed upright. I dug with my paddle to get her nose pointed proper downstream.

And then we were going, rocking and bobbing down the river toward my horse.

The leaves on the riverbank trees were changing and were all a-glory in their fall colors. The river was bubbling and chattering, telling a story about hope and adventure. The hills around us had just a frosting of snow on their tops. Just the down of the angels' wings, maybe.

For the first time in a long time, I felt like I was finally getting a break.

For the first time in a long time, I felt like I was getting closer to my sweet Sarah.

CHAPTER
13

That dugout Indian canoe was sure enough sturdy, but it weren't at all easy to steer. It bounced and jolted down the river any way it pleased—Ah-Kee and I were just along for the ride, holding on tight.

The Yakima Canyon was one of the purtiest darn places I'd ever seen. The hills were piled up on either side and the river shot right through it, rambling from side to side on the valley floor. In some places the hills came right down to the water, pinching the river between. In other places the valley floor spread out, and we saw cabins and homesteads nestled between the mountains and the riverbed. The whole place was dotted with trees, all different sorts: aspens shaking their leaves in the wind, broad-leaf trees all covered in orange and red, and plenty of sturdy pines with their evergreen needles ready for winter. We rounded one bend and came across a herd of big, brown elk, crossing the river. They scooted along quick when they saw our tree-sized boat coming down their way.

"This place seems like some kind of heaven," I said, turning back to Ah-Kee. He looked at me and cocked his head curiously. So I just spread my arms, taking in the scene, and shot him a big, head-shaking smile. He understood. He nodded and smiled back at me, and said a few words in Chinese.

I couldn't help wishing that Papa and I had tried to homestead here, instead. There'd a been no trip over the Colockum, no overturned wagon, and Papa'd still be here. We'd be living here in heaven, close enough to visit Mama and Katie's graves when we wanted. The thought was too sad to hold on to for long; I had to let it go and leave it behind in the water. Maybe that was a story the river could tell to someone else. It wouldn't seem sad to them if they didn't know it never happened.

We made good time down the river, through that canyon. My neck almost hurt from looking around at all that pretty, and my heart surged with a hopeful beat as I felt the miles between me and Sarah falling away.

The first rough patch we hit gave us both a scare. We heard the roar coming before we got there. Then the river tightened down to an angry channel of white water and black rocks. The boat struck a big rock, then another, jolting from side to side and darn near throwing me out. Water—ice cold and shocking—splashed up, blurring my eyes and drenching my clothes. We started drifting sideways in the river, and I remembered Jed Holcomb's warning to keep the nose pointed downstream. As the canoe swung slowly to the side, I could tell why: If we hit a rock or got jammed up like that, the boat would flip Ah-Kee and me right into the water for sure.

"Straight!" I shouted back to Ah-Kee. "We gotta keep her straight!" I made a straight up-and-down motion with my arm, showing how we had to point downriver. Ah-Kee nodded and shouted something back and we both worked with our paddles, straining together to keep the boat true through the rapids. The canoe was like a bucking horse, dropping hard and then jumping up, skipping to the side. I fought to stay on my knees, and had to switch quick between paddling and just plain holding on, then back again when we started going crooked.

Then we were through, back to calm waters and sunshine scenery. I shivered and tried to catch my breath, then looked back at Ah-Kee to make sure he was still in the boat.

His face looked a lot like what I felt: scared and relieved and thrilled and cold to my bones.

Then a big, toothy grin cracked across his face, so big it almost closed his eyes. He lifted his paddle triumphantly and shouted something high and excited.

"Yeah," I laughed back at him, wiping the water out of my eyes. "I guess that was kinda fun, Ah-Kee. But truth be told, I could go for a little less fun, if it's all right with you."

We shot through a few more rapids, doing a little better every time. I felt like we were sure enough getting the hang of it. There were a few times where the water was so low the bottom of the canoe scraped on the river-bottom stones, and we had to hop out and push it free. Between that and the splashing rapids, we were pretty well drenched from head to toe and feeling the October breeze that was blowing off the mountains.

Then, from up ahead, I heard it. The roar of rapids coming up . . . but bigger, deeper, and louder than any we'd come through before. I stretched up tall to try and get a look. I could see where it started—a mess of rocks, a flashing froth of white water spitting up and splashing—but then the river dropped down and I couldn't see the end of it. But I could feel the roaring rumble of those rapids in my chest.

Paddling would be useless. We were at the river's mercy, and it sure weren't looking all that merciful. I threw my paddle down in the bottom of the boat, grabbed on to the sides with both hands, and prayed that Ah-Kee was doing the same behind me.

"Ah-Kee!" I screamed at the top of my lungs. "Get ready! Get ready!"

And then we were in it, flying faster than my thoughts or senses could keep up with.

We shot this way and that, bumping and jarring and flying and dropping. All I could hear or feel or see was water roaring and water splashing. Then the boat hit a boulder; it tipped dangerously, almost all the way over. My fingers burned gripping that wet canoe, and my face went down low to the water, black and hungry and waiting for me. I screamed a scream of sure enough terror, and heard Ah-Kee screaming behind me, too. But then the boat righted and we swung wildly back on course. I risked a quick look back and saw Ah-Kee still on board with me, dripping wet and wide-eyed, knuckles white on the boat's sides.

We careened crazily from one heart attack to the next, without a moment to catch our breath between. Our boat was held tight in the river's fist, and it squeezed and shook us like dice.

We were almost to the end, though; the nose of the boat

flew up high and I could see the easy water ahead, running polite and calm as you please through the canyon. There was only one twisting drop left, but I didn't like the look of it. There was a furious flurry of white water before us, then that vicious turning drop between two boulders taller than me, and a graveyard of sharp rocks waiting at the bottom. Just beyond the rocks, right before that smooth water I was eager to get to, was a big mess of a logjam, spanning almost the whole river. Just the thing Jed Holcomb had warned us about.

"All right, Ah-Kee," I hollered. "Hold on now, by Go—"

But then we were in it, and my words got swept away by the wild river.

If the earlier rapids had been like riding a runaway horse, the last stretch was sure enough a stampeding herd of buffalo.

Ah-Kee and I never stood a chance.

We flew one way, then the other, then hit the big plunge between the boulders. The nose of the boat went over and we hung there a second, floating amidst all that chaos; then we dropped. It was too steep, almost straight down. The nose stabbed down into the water and stuck like an arrow and me and Ah-Kee went flying head over heels into the frigid water, right atop each other.

Before we could get our bearings, we were being carried downstream, heads coming up and then going back under, legs and arms all a-tangle. I got spun backward and smashed into a rock, sending jolts of pain up my back. Ah-Kee started to scream and then went under, his shout cutting off in a wet choke.

My satchel hung heavy around my neck, weighing me down, but I wouldn't cut it loose. It held all the money I had left; the money I needed to get Sarah back. I tried to kick my arms and legs as best as I could but the water was too fast and I was already half-numb from the cold. I spit out a mouthful of water and gasped a full lungs-worth of air before being pulled back under and swept farther downstream.

Somewhere down there, in the swirling icy blackness, I felt Ah-Kee bump up against me. He was floating still and motionless and my whole sorry self shivered and cried out.

Then I felt his arms move and grab hold of me, felt his fingers tighten around my coat, and I did the same, holding tight onto him down there in the murderous water.

We came up together, coughing and gasping, facing downstream. I was surprised when my feet hit the solid bottom of the river and I got my footing beneath me, still clutching Ah-Kee. I was almost steady, almost standing firm in all that moving water, when a train locomotive smashed into me from behind. My body exploded in pain, and I was pushed down and under, and I felt rough wood scraping down my back, holding me beneath the water. That heavy Indian dugout canoe had caught up and crashed into me.

I popped up to the side of it and threw one arm up inside, grateful to finally have something to hold on to. I sucked great gasping breaths of air and looked for Ah-Kee. My eyes found his head bobbing up and down a little ahead and off to the side. He was keeping easily afloat; it looked like he knew how to swim after all. My breath slowed down and my heart started to calm, figuring the worst was behind us.

That's when I remembered the logjam. I craned my head around and saw it coming up fast, an ugly snarl of limbs and trees and logs growing out from either bank and cutting right across the river. The logs were like vicious crooked teeth, with the water pouring through; if a body got pressed up against those teeth, there'd be no getting out alive. There was only one narrow path in the middle of the logjam, where the two sides didn't quite meet up; me and the boat were floating straight for it. But Ah-Kee was bound right for the deadly mass of logs. He was facing me, his back to the doom he was coming up on.

"Ah-Kee!" I shouted. "Ah-Kee!"

He smiled and waved, no doubt as happy to be out of the rapids as I had been a moment before.

"No!" I screamed, pointing frantically past him. "Swim, Ah-Kee! Swim!"

His head turned and he saw the trouble he was in and started to paddle furiously, clumsily, toward the bank. But it was clear he'd never make it that far before the river pinned him to the logjam and swallowed him whole.

"No! To the middle, Ah-Kee!" I waved him in with my free arm. "To the middle! Swim to me!"

He looked desperately toward me and then changed

direction, beating his arms in the water to try and reach me before it was too late.

But I saw with a terrible certainty that it was impossible. Ah-Kee was going to be crushed into the logjam; Ah-Kee was going to be lost.

Then I remembered something terrible, and wonderful: Ezra Bishop's whip.

I still wore it wrapped around my shoulder. I slipped it off over my neck, holding as best as I could to the thick handle with my cold-deadened hand.

"Grab hold!" I shouted, and whipped that black leather monster out across the water toward him. It was sure enough long, a good fifteen feet from handle to tip.

The end slapped the water a few feet from where he struggled, and with one frantic kick he reached it and grabbed tight with both hands. I pulled with all the strength I had left in my shoulders, then slid my hand forward on the whip and hauled it in again.

On the other end Ah-Kee was doing the same, pulling himself up that whip hand over hand.

I saw those logs sure enough reaching for him, saw his face, terrified and straining with all he had in him, heard the thirsty slurp of the water trying to suck us both down, and then I yanked right down to the very bottom of myself and he surged through the water closer toward me.

I thought he was gonna make it. I truly did.

I truly thought that I'd pulled him far enough with that

cursed whip for him to float clear of the logs and safe through the gap.

But we were just short.

Ah-Kee was bobbing closer then he stopped fast, snagged by a nasty broken-off stump jutting out from a fallen tree. In half a breath, before I could do any darned thing, I shot right past him, through the gap of clear water in the middle of the jam.

He cried out, stuck there on that weathered white stump, as I went past. Then I was gone.

"No!" I screamed.

I looked back just in time to see the whip go taut and snap out of the water, tight as wire between us. It almost yanked me right off the boat but I kept my grip tight, on the boat and the whip both. At the same moment, Ah-Kee let out one last desperate shout and he went down, under the log. Under the water.

I hung stuck for a second, almost pulled in two by the boat pulling me downriver and the whip holding me upstream.

Then the whip went slack.

Me and the boat took to floating downstream again, through the peaceful waters past the rapids. I hung off the side, breathless. I forgot all about the cold, all about the wet. All about anything but the empty river behind me and the loose whip in my hand, binding me to nothing but black water.

I heard the honking of geese, flying south above me in a sloppy V in the sky.

All around me was the blaze of changing leaves, shouting their colors as they died.

Tears, burning hot in all the coldness, sprang to my eyes.

"Oh, God," I said as a chill shook me to my bones. "Oh, God, I—"

And then Ah-Kee's head popped up and his wild gulping breath shattered all the stillness that had gathered around me.

"Ah-Kee!" I hollered. "Ah-Kee!" And then I whooped a wild whoop, a joyous whoop like had never rung out of my lungs before.

Ah-Kee sputtered and coughed and gasped. I kicked to slow the boat and he churned his way toward me and then he grabbed hold of the canoe and threw his head back, eyes closed and mouth still gasping all that sweet, living air. I hugged him good and hard, as tight as I could without drowning him again or letting go of the boat. I had sure enough thought he was dead, and it had been just about more than I could take.

I threw the whip up in the boat—eternally grateful that Ezra Bishop was a brutal man and that I was a thief—and together Ah-Kee and I kicked the boat toward the shore. When we were in water shallow enough for walking, we dragged it up until its nose sat on dry land and it was clear it wasn't going anywhere. I saw one paddle floating past and I splashed out and grabbed it and threw it in the boat. The other was lost for good, but I was certainly thankful that a paddle was all we'd lost that day.

Ah-Kee and I stood on the shore, shivering. The river ran before us, unbothered by the near tragedy that had just occurred. I opened my satchel, still hanging soggily against my side. Papa's pistol would need cleaning, but the money was all still there. So was the knife, and some strips of elk jerky that Jed Holcomb had given us. I pulled my matches out. They were dripping wet, and I knew they were useless.

"We need to get dry," I told Ah-Kee, my teeth chattering. "These wet clothes will be the death of us."

I turned away from the river, scanning the forest for help. The woods around us looked wild and unsettled, but then I saw it: a steady wisp of smoke, rising in a column above the trees not too far from where we were.

"Come on, Ah-Kee," I said, and took off at a jog.

We found a rugged dirt road winding through the trees and followed it parallel to the river for a ways, then turned off on a smaller, even rougher path that climbed up toward where I'd seen the smoke.

We came out of the trees into a clearing and there sat a log cabin, sturdy and tidy, with a neat little front porch and firewood stacked tightly up against the side. A small creek ran down past it toward the river. In the back I could see a stable, and a corral where a cow was grazing. It looked at us as we walked up, chewing calmly at the cud in its mouth. It was a fine little scene, that cabin sitting there with the meadow and mountains behind it. The kinda scene that a fella could almost feel homesick for, even if he'd never been there before. Me and Ah-Kee were both shivering something fierce, and I hoped the folks inside were as friendly as their cabin looked.

I did my best to wring the worst of the water out of my shirt, then knocked on the door.

It swung open so fast and so sudden I jumped back.

A boy was standing there, fear all over his face. He weren't no more than five years old. His eyes looked ready to cry.

"You the doctor?" he cried, looking back and forth between me and Ah-Kee.

"Doctor?" I said back. I looked at Ah-Kee, standing slack-jawed beside me. Then my own twelve-year-old self, dripping wet and shivering. "*No*, kid. Not even *close*."

"Oh, Lord!" the boy wailed. His face crumpled and tears streamed from his eyes and down his face. His shoulders shook with sobs.

"What's the matter?" I asked, stepping forward. Then again, "What's the matter?"

He sniffed and looked up at me, his face a picture of heartbreak and misery.

"My mama," he gasped. "She's hurt! My mama's gonna die!"

Well, me? I'd seen enough of mamas dying. I didn't waste no time.

"Where is she at?" I asked him.

He stepped to the side. I waited only long enough to take off my mud-caked boots, then walked into the cabin.

"Mama! Mama!" he whispered loudly. "Look what I brought!"

I took a few steps into the cabin, letting my eyes adjust to the darkness. Ah-Kee followed behind.

The inside of the cabin was cozy, with a stone fireplace and a table and stove and some plain pieces of furniture here and there. It had a real plank floor, level and swept clean. In the corner was a big pine bed, and in the bed was a woman. Her face was pale, her eyes dark and exhausted, and her straight brown hair was wet with sweat, but I could tell even then that she was a pretty woman.

Her eyes were swimming in pain but she squinted and saw us and I saw confusion wrinkle her brow. But she smiled, a tired and hurting smile.

"Oh," she said. Her voice was weak, but I could tell she was trying her best to be warm. "Hello. Who . . . are you?"

Standing there breathless in dripping wet clothes, I wasn't sure how to answer.

"My name's Joseph, ma'am. This here's Ah-Kee. Your boy here says you're hurt?"

"Hurt?" The woman grimaced in pain and waited a moment. "Hurt's not the right word." She gritted her teeth and paused again. "I'm having a baby, you see. Any minute, I believe."

CHAPTER
14

ou're having a baby?" My voice came out high and nervous-sounding. If I was to make a list of all the things I wasn't likely to be much help in doing, delivering a baby would be right up near the top.

"Yes. It's been working on coming for two days now. My husband left to fetch the doctor this morning, and—" Her voice cut off in a gasp and she arched her back and ground her teeth and closed her eyes against the pain.

"Mama!" the little boy cried out, and he ran to her side and took her hand. I stood there dripping in the doorway, not sure what to do. I turned to Ah-Kee, thinking maybe we ought to step outside for privacy's sake, when he brushed right past me and walked over to the bed.

I stood there staring, open-mouthed.

Ah-Kee walked straight up to that woman and started talking, just like he had to that grizzly, his voice calm and easy and reassuring. The woman and the boy looked up at him, no doubt stupefied. When he'd said his piece he did a quick bow to her.

"What did he say?" the woman asked.

"I don't have the slightest idea, ma'am," I answered honestly.

Ah-Kee looked around and walked over to the table and fetched a pitcher of water and a cloth, then returned to the bed. He soaked the cloth in the water, squeezed it out, then pressed it up against the woman's forehead.

I saw her body relax, and she closed her eyes and smiled.

"Thank you," she said. But just as quick her whole body tightened again and she bucked and moaned through clenched teeth. The boy started crying again, quiet, just breathing loud through his nose with tears tumbling out of his eyes.

Ah-Kee looked back at me and barked some sort of order in Chinese.

I shook my head and shrugged.

He did some more talking and pointed at a pot by the fire, then at a bucket sitting by me near the door, and I got the message. Soon I had a pot of water set to boil over the fire. Ah-Kee had gone around the cabin and gathered any cloths or towels or blankets he could find, and had propped the woman up into more of a sitting position in the bed.

"Joseph?" she whispered to me while Ah-Kee was busy over by the fire. "Does he know what he's doing?"

I gave her the most confident look I could muster.

"Ma'am," I said, "I've been traveling with that boy for a few days and lots of miles now. And about the only thing I haven't seen him be able to do is hold on to a horse. I'd reckon that, somehow or other, he knows exactly what he's doing."

She nodded, then screwed her eyes shut against another rush of pain. Beads of sweat popped out on her forehead. She grabbed my hand and squeezed it sure enough hard, so hard I was reasonably certain the next sound I was gonna hear would be my bones snapping. Then the pain passed, and she looked at me and gave me an apologetic smile.

"My name's Anna, by the way," she said, still breathing

shallow though her pale lips. "Anna Davidson. This is my son, Justin." Justin nodded at me solemnly and stuck out his hand and I shook it.

"I suppose . . . I should ask you . . ." Mrs. Davidson's words came in bits and pieces, between the moments of pain. "What it is . . . you two boys . . . are doing here."

I thought of our whole wild story, of Sarah and Mr. Grissom and Ezra Bishop and Colockum Pass and running the river and Mr. Campbell heading into Yakima. But then Mrs. Davidson squeezed my hand and cried out a real honest-to-goodness scream, and I knew that it all could wait. All of it. It would have to wait. Even me and Sarah.

I waited 'til she calmed, then I said, "Ma'am, we are trying to catch up to my Sarah. But that ain't important right now. All you gotta know is that us two boys are doing nothing here but our best to help you and yours. We can sort out all the rest later."

"Aren't your ma and pa waiting on you somewhere?"

I bit my lip.

"No, ma'am. They are not. And Ah-Kee and I ain't going nowhere 'til you're all right." And I didn't have to listen in my heart for Mama and Papa's words to know I was doing the right thing.

She squeezed my hand but this time it weren't out of pain, but gratitude.

"Thank you," she whispered. Then the pain came. And it came again. And it didn't let up.

That baby was a hard time coming. I hadn't never seen a soul in as much struggle as Mrs. Davidson, and right then I hoped I never would again.

After an especially bad bout of pain, she looked into my eyes and whispered, "This baby ain't comin' easy, Joseph. Please talk to me. Give me something to listen to."

I cleared my throat, licked my lips, and cast about in my mind for words to say to her.

"My . . . my mama told me that I was quite a trial when I was born," I began. "I laid her flat for three days. She said she thought I'd be the death of her. It used to make me feel all kinds of terrible guilty. But then she said that babies that come into the world difficult are the ones you're most grateful for, and that they are bound for great things." I paused, looking at the sweat dripping down the sides of her face. "If that's the case, ma'am, then, well, I reckon this little baby is sure enough gonna be president of these United States someday."

Mrs. Davidson smiled at me, just for a second.

"Thank you," she breathed. "Keep talking?"

The morning turned to afternoon out the cabin's one framed window, then to the golden colors of evening, then right on into darkness. Justin and I sat up by Mrs. Davidson's head the whole time, holding her hands and pressing cold cloths to her forehead and doing anything else Ah-Kee had us do. And I talked. I talked myself hoarse. I told her about our life before we came out west. I told her about my little Katie being born, how it had snowed up to the middle of the wagon wheels and the doctor couldn't come and Mama had birthed her all on her own. I told her about the time Katie and I snuck into Mama's sugar sack and ate ourselves sick and got a whipping for it to boot. I told her about the time Papa had tried to surprise Mama by making her cornbread for her birthday, but he'd burned it so bad we'd had to eat outside on account of the smoke in the house. I told her about learning to ride Sarah, and teaching Katie to ride her, too. I told Mrs. Davidson all the stories of my life and my family.

Well, almost all. I didn't tell her the sad ones. A birth ain't no place to bring sadness to. So I didn't tell her how Katie's story ended, or my papa's, or my mama's. I kept those to myself, where they belonged.

And all the while, Ah-Kee worked like a sure enough real-life angel. He never stopped moving all those dark and trying hours. And his voice was always steady. And his eyes were always calm. And he always gave Anna Davidson a little smile, just when she needed it most.

I don't know where Ah-Kee learned how to birth a baby. Maybe his mama back in China was a midwife, and he went along. Maybe in Chinese camps there's no doctor and every-one pitches in. I don't know. I s'pose I'll never know. But Ah-Kee knew every minute exactly what to do, right down to the end. And he did it.

That boy was a wonder.

When finally the moment came, it was like all the mira-cles in the world happened at once. Mrs. Davidson was gripping my hand, the veins in her neck popping out as she pushed and hollered. Justin was holding her other hand, his eyes wide and wet and desperate.

The world out the window was dark but inside we had the flickering light of the fire. And the steady flame of an oil lamp. And Ah-Kee's quiet, strong voice holding us together. And then we had the first, pure cry of a newborn baby.

And then, just right then, from out of nowhere, big hot tears sprung into my eyes and then came pouring out down my cheeks. Wet, flowing, unstoppable tears from some deep place in my heart.

It could've been that I was remembering my dear little Katie being born, the sound of her first cries and seeing her little red body and knowing I was a big brother. It could have been just the exhaustion, the hours of effort and fear finally coming to a happy ending. Or it could have been Anna Davidson's smile, after hours of pain and sweat and struggle, a smile that was so tired but so complete and so shot-through with triumph and joy and a tender, fierce kind of love. The love of a mama. A love unlike any other. A love I so sorely missed. And always will. But standing there in that cabin, I ain't one bit ashamed to say I cried good, wet tears that were all happy. I cried them for that baby, and that mama, and maybe for all babies and all mamas. Me and mine included.

Ah-Kee handed the child to Mrs. Davidson, wrapped in a towel.

"Oh, my baby," she said softly, stroking its little cheek

with a gentle finger. "My baby." And that baby stopped crying and just lay there with its mama, eyes closed.

"What is it, Mama?" Justin asked, his voice hushed and breathless, his wide eyes on the baby's tiny face.

"It's a girl, Justin," she answered. "A sister."

"A sister? Golly."

"What do you think of her, sweetie? What do you think of your new sister?"

Their voices were soft and secret, the warm special voices of a family. They talked to just each other and the baby, like Ah-Kee and I weren't even there.

"I like her, Mama. I like her just fine." But it was clear from the shaking hush in his voice that Justin more than just liked his sister. He was sure enough in awe of her.

The cabin felt suddenly too hot. Too tight.

I excused myself quickly and stepped out into the wide open coolness of the night.

The air was a deep kind of cold, the sort of cold that tells your bones that fall is ending and winter is coming right up behind it. A mostly full moon threw its silver light on the snow-topped hills, the pines, the grass around the cabin. Off in the distance I could hear the river, tumbling its way through the night toward Yakima.

I stood alone in the darkness. Well, with the moon it weren't all-the-way darkness. But I felt sure enough all-the-way alone.

I wanted my horse back right then more than ever.

CHAPTER
15

The ax head shined bright as a bullet in the morning light. It glinted as it rose up, swift and deadly, then flashed as it came slicing down. I grunted and gasped. My aim was true and the log split in half, falling to the ground in two even pieces.

I stopped to rest, catching my breath. I looked at the wood I'd chopped, added to the pile beside the cabin. The sun was high up in the cloudless blue sky. I was wearing some of the absent Mr. Davidson's clothes, while mine and Ah-Kee's hung drying on a line. Morning was well gone, and my belly was asking about lunch. I threw the last two pieces on the stack, grabbed the bucket and the basket I'd put by the door, and headed inside.

Mrs. Davidson was lying in bed, feeding the baby.

"No more work, Joseph," she said. "Between the animals and the wood and the cleaning, you've done more than enough. Come sit over here and talk to me." She spoke softly. Ah-Kee and Justin were both asleep—Justin on his own little bed, Ah-Kee in a pile of blankets on the floor, plum tuckered out from the long night of birthing. I'd woken up restless and hadn't stopped moving since. I walked over and sat on the chair by Mrs. Davidson's bed.

"Have you picked out a name yet?" I asked her.

"I think I have," she said with a smile. "Claire. Claire Marie Davidson. Claire was my mother's name. What do you think?"

"I think that's a fine name."

"Would you like to hold her?"

I swallowed and looked at Claire, now lying asleep in her

mama's lap. I remembered my own Katie, the light fragile feel of her.

"Sure, ma'am. I s'pose I could hold her a bit."

"Have you held a baby before?"

"Yes, ma'am. My sister." Mrs. Davidson held Claire out, and I took the warm little bundle into my arms and held her strong but soft against me.

"Oh, of course! How old is your sister now, Joseph?"

"She was six, ma'am."

"Was?"

"She passed away last year. Typhoid." I kept my voice gentle and easy. To keep the baby calm. "My mama, too."

I could feel Mrs. Davidson's eyes on me. But I didn't look up. I didn't want to move, didn't want to wake the baby.

After a moment, she spoke again.

"Do you have any other brothers or sisters? Or is it just you and your papa?"

"No, ma'am. My papa died this spring." I kept my voice at a whisper, my eyes on the baby sleeping in my arms. "It is just me."

It felt like a bad secret. Like a shame. I don't know why. But I was afraid for some reason that when Mrs. Davidson found out about me, that she'd want me to leave. Maybe it's an orphan thing. Since Papa died, no matter where I was, I felt like I didn't belong there. And no matter who I was with, I felt like I didn't belong with them. And I guess I was afraid they felt the same thing—that I didn't belong there.

"Me and Ah-Kee will leave as soon as he wakes up," I said. "We'll get outta your way and let you care for this baby."

I couldn't look up at her. I didn't know what I'd see in her eyes.

"No," she answered me. "No, Joseph, you will not be leaving soon. You and Ah-Kee came here like angels—like *angels*, Joseph, answering my prayers—and you are staying for dinner and a night's rest and forever after, if you want."

Forever after had a funny sound to it. A good funny sound. My throat got tight, and I let it loosen a bit before I spoke again.

"Thank you, ma'am, but we can't stay."

"Why not?"

Mrs. Davidson and me both jumped and looked over to where Justin was sitting up in his bed. He crawled out and walked over to us, rubbing at his eyes, his hair all sleep-crooked.

"I think you *should* stay here forever with us! Why can't you?"

I sighed. It was a long story. But I s'posed I had to tell it to them.

"Well," I began, "I've got to get my horse back, you see."

By the time I was done telling everything right up to where Ah-Kee and I washed up cold and shivering on the riverbank, Ah-Kee was awake, too. He sat and listened, and smiled every time his name came into it. When I motioned for him to, he pulled out his bird carving and showed it to them.

"And that's it," I finished. "My Sarah is over in Yakima, and I've got to get to her before she's gone for good. And I know Ah-Kee is sure keen to find whatever it is he's looking for."

Mrs. Davidson and Justin sat staring at us.

"That's quite a story," Mrs. Davidson finally said.

"I s'pose it is, ma'am."

"I hope you get her back," Justin said.

"Thank you," I said back with a smile. "Me, too. So I best be getting along now."

"Right now?" Justin asked, his voice high with alarm.

"Well, yeah, I mean—"

"But Pa ain't home yet! You're gonna leave us here alone?"

I looked down into his big, scared-kid eyes.

"Now, Justin, you heard him. He's got to go. We'll be fine here."

But Justin ignored his mama and grabbed ahold of my leg.

"Please, Joseph, don't go yet. Don't leave us alone."

I bit my lip. I felt his fingers tight on my leg, felt that sleeping Claire snug against me. I sure enough knew something about being left alone.

"All right," I said at last. "Another day ain't gonna hurt us. We'll leave first thing in the morning."

Justin whooped and beamed a whole-face kind of smile. He squeezed my leg in a tight hug, and I reckoned right then it was worth it.

*   *   *

Mr. Davidson got home that afternoon, worn out and about dying with worry. He ran up ragged, pulling a horse lathered in sweat. His eyes were almost black from lack of sleep, and his face was pale and wasted. He strode inside, passing Ah-Kee and me on the porch without a glance, and went right up to Mrs. Davidson, who was lying in bed nursing the baby. We started following him but held back in the doorway, out of respect.

"Dr. Fowler was gone," he gasped, falling to his knees at her bedside. "I had to go all the way to Yakima."

"It's all right, John," Mrs. Davidson said softly.

"But that damned doctor wouldn't come all this way," he continued as though he hadn't heard her. "He wouldn't come." He shook his head. "Then ol' Buck threw a shoe and got a nasty cut on his hoof, and I had to walk him all the way back."

"It's all right, John," she murmured again. She pulled back the blanket, showing the face of that newborn baby girl. "I'm all right. *She's* all right."

Mr. Davidson reached out, tender and slow, and ran a finger along that little girl's cheek. There was a hushed sort of moment, full and warm, as daddy met daughter and daughter met daddy.

"She's beautiful," he said at last, and his voice was hoarse.

"Yes," said Mrs. Davidson.

"And she *is* all right."

"Yes," she said again. Then she smiled, and nodded toward Ah-Kee and me in the door. "Thanks to them."

Mr. Davidson turned to look at us, and his eyes narrowed

in exhausted confusion. Mrs. Davidson told him, in her warm and almost humming voice, about our arrival and the birth of the baby and all the wonders Ah-Kee had done.

When the tale was told, Mr. Davidson rose to his feet and walked over to us. He looked us each in the eye, clear and strong, and shook our hands, and gave us each a firm and steady "thank you."

I liked how he did it for Ah-Kee just the same as he did it for me. I liked how he gave my friend that respect. It wasn't a lot to give, but from what I'd seen so far in our travels, I knew that plenty wouldn't have given it.

"You fellas," he said next, and I also liked how he didn't call us boys, "are welcome to stay here as long as you need and as long as you like."

"Thank you, sir," I answered. "But it'll just be the night. We've got business to attend to, Ah-Kee and me."

Mr. Davidson squinted wearily at us, two rumpled and travel-stained boys.

"Business?" he said. "That sounds like a story. Let's get dinner on the table and hear it."

So I told my whole story again over a dinner of warmed-up salt ham and some passable biscuits baked up by Mr. Davidson himself.

"Do you miss your sister?" Justin asked me when I was done. He was looking at little baby Claire when he asked.

"Justin," Mrs. Davidson admonished him.

"It's all right, ma'am." I turned to Justin. " 'Course I miss her. Something awful. We were close, me and Katie. Real close. She . . . she never just called me Joseph. She always called me, '*my Joseph*.' I don't know why. But I was always *her* Joseph." My voice trailed off and left the table in silence.

Justin squinted at me.

"Well . . . whose Joseph are you now, then?"

I looked at him.

"I don't know," I answered after a moment. "Nobody's, I guess."

There was a silence, heavy and waiting. Like a fruit ripening on a tree.

"You can be my Joseph, if you want," he offered.

"Thanks," I said, after a moment and a swallow. "That sounds fine."

That night Justin insisted I sleep in his bed with him. The bed was just big enough for the both of us, with him lying tight up against me. It reminded me of lying with Katie. We whispered together in the darkness, just like Katie and I had.

"Why you gotta get that horse so bad, Joseph?"

I considered his question.

"Well, what's the most precious thing in the world to you?" I asked. "The thing you love the most?"

Justin thought for a second.

"Well, I guess it'd be Claire. Is a sister a good answer?"

I smiled, thinking of my own dear Katie, but I couldn't keep a bit of sadness outta my voice when I answered.

"Sure it is. That's a fine answer. Now, if someone took Claire away and was getting farther and farther away, and it was up to you to find her and bring her back safe, would you?"

" 'Course I would! I'd go all the way around the world if I had to!"

"That's what I reckoned. Well, my horse is like that for me. She's my Claire, and she's all I got. You understand?"

I felt him nod beside me.

"I just hope I find her," I said softly. "I hope I get her back."

Justin sat up, then put his head down on my chest. He lay there for a second and then he spoke.

"You are. You are gonna find her. I can tell."

"How can you tell?"

"It's your heart. It don't beat right. Hearts always go like this: *ba-pum, ba-pum*. But with yours I can only hear the *pums*, not the *ba's*. You're missing half your heart. I bet you your horse has got the other half. That means you *gotta* find her, so's you'll have one whole heart again. I know it."

I don't know if I smiled or not when he said that. In the dark it's hard to tell sometimes. But I know I liked what he'd said. There was a sure enough sort of truth in it, I reckoned.

*　　*　　*

In the early morning darkness, the angels and devils hour, Ah-Kee and I stood by the boat with Mr. Davidson. Mrs. Davidson and Justin and Claire were asleep back in the cabin. The world was cold, but the sun was coming.

Mr. Davidson was a good man. I'd been able to tell right away. He was quiet, but he was good and sturdy. He reminded me, in some ways, of my own papa.

Before I got in the boat, he put a hand on my shoulder.

"You're a fine boy, son. And you'll be a heckuva man someday. Your papa and mama would be mighty proud of you, I promise."

My eyes burned in the frosty morning air and I looked away.

"You know that you'd always be welcome here. When you get that horse of yours back, or even if you don't, we'd always have a place for you. A boy like you, such a hard worker and good with animals, you'd be a real blessing to us. Ah-Kee, too, of course. This could be home for you, Joseph."

I nodded. Mrs. Davidson had told me the same thing the day before.

I thought of the little cabin with its winter woodpile, nestled snug in the hills that tumbled down to the river. I thought of the fine people inside: the mama, that miracle of a baby, the hard-hugging boy, and this steady man before me. If I were to pick a home, I couldn't think of a finer one. It tugged at my heart and burrowed down into me like a bird into a nest.

But in this life, I s'pose, we don't get to pick our homes.

"I appreciate that, sir. I do. But I reckon I don't know where I'll end up. Maybe home just ain't something I'm meant to have."

He squeezed my shoulder, then let go and held his hand out to me. I took it, and then Ah-Kee did the same.

A shiver shook my shoulders. The air was bitter cold around me.

Mr. Davidson saw it. His eyes sharpened.

"I felt like I had to give you boys something," he said. I started to shake my head, but he stopped me with a look that was serious and unbending. "I knew you wouldn't take money and, frankly, I ain't got none to give. But I can give you this."

He reached up and unwound the black scarf he'd wrapped around his neck before leaving the cabin. It was short but thick, and warm, knit from coarse and sturdy wool.

"My mama made this," he said, handing it to me. "It'll keep you warm, and I know she'd be happy for you to have it."

"Thank you," I said, and tied it around my neck.

Then he pulled the hat from his head, knit snug and tight from a dark green yarn.

"Anna made this," he said as he pressed it into Ah-Kee's hands. "It's yours, now. Thank you, for everything."

Ah-Kee bowed, and pulled the hat over his head. I know we were both grateful for the gifts, and the warmth they gave us. Mr. Davidson gave us one more nod, then helped us into the boat.

He looked at us a moment, sitting there together in that canoe in the near darkness. He shook his head, a small smile playing across his lips.

"You boys. You got some kind of courage. Both of you. Yes, sir. Now go get what you're after."

With that he gave the canoe a hard shove, sending us out away from the bank and into the waiting current.

"Good luck, boys," he called out as we drifted away toward sunrise.

CHAPTER
16

There was a sadness in leaving that happy home, in saying good-bye again to that familiar feeling of family that I missed so much. But it was sure enough good to be moving again, to see the trees drifting past as me and Ah-Kee once again pointed our faces in the direction we were going and *went*.

Sunlight was hitting the tops of the trees as the sun peeked over the canyon's mountain walls, and birds were trying out their morning songs. The world was waking up all around us and we were getting closer again, I hoped, to my Sarah.

There were no more bone-shaking rapids, no more swimming for me and Ah-Kee. There were some logjams we had to steer around with our paddle, there were some runs we had to hold tight and pray, but that morning the river seemed to be on our side. She carried us on, out of the canyon and into the wide-open sunshine of Yakima Valley.

The town of Yakima was pretty big, at least compared to what I was used to. As we floated up to it we went under bridges that were busy with wagons and horses and people on the move. It was harvest time, after all, and all the orchards were busy getting their apples and pears picked and out to market. The town itself was a sprawl of wooden houses and businesses around a downtown of a few taller brick buildings. From the river we could hear voices, the whinnies of horses, and the hissing and clanking of a train coming or going.

I set my jaw in determination. It was a big town to find one horse in, or one man. And I was a day behind now. The morning's sunshine faded as we got closer, and clouds crowded the sky. A chilling wind blew through my old clothes. A storm was coming for sure.

Me and Ah-Kee ran our boat up into the bank under some trees and hopped ashore, then headed on into town.

The streets were muddy and jostling with the traffic of horses, wagons, and men. When we got to the middle of town, an intersection of two streets with brick buildings all around, we just stopped and stood there a minute. I didn't know where to start.

Ah-Kee was standing beside me, gaping at all the commotion just like I was. He looked even smaller and more alone than I felt. I took a step closer to him. Then I smiled at him and nodded, and he nodded back, and I got down to business.

"Excuse me, sir?" I asked the first man I saw, walking down the road with a newspaper under his arm. "I'm looking for a horse trader by the name of Mr. Campbell."

The man frowned at me, then looked at Ah-Kee and his frown deepened into a downright scowl. He brushed past us without saying a word.

Mama said that if someone's putting ugliness into the world, you can't be ugly back; you gotta put a little bit of sunshine into the world to even things out.

I looked at Ah-Kee, who was looking up at me. I made my

best imitation of the man, screwing my face up into an exaggerated, evil-looking scowl. Ah-Kee looked confused for a second, then his face cracked into a smile and he laughed. I reckoned that was a little bit of sunshine.

There weren't no point in giving up. Ah-Kee and I walked up that street, with me asking anyone I could about Mr. Campbell. Some folks were rude, but most folks just said they didn't know the man or where to find him. A cold rain started dripping down, and the street mostly emptied out. I felt my horse slipping away from me.

Finally we found our luck.

A fine-looking man in a suit, hurrying into a building, answered, "Campbell? No, son, I'm afraid I don't." I was prepared to thank him and move on when he added, "But if you keep going down that way you'll get to Smithson's. He's a farrier and horse trader himself, probably the biggest in Yakima. If this Campbell fellow came through here looking for horses, I'd wager that Smithson would know about it."

"Thank you, sir! Thank you!" I grabbed Ah-Kee by the hand, and we took off running down the street through the rain that was picking and pecking at us.

Smithson's had a big sign out front: SMITHSON'S SADDLE & TACK: FARRIER, DEALER, HORSES BOUGHT & SOLD. It was a wooden building with a display window full of saddles and bridles, with a big stable and corral out back.

I rushed inside and right past the saddles and displays and goods, to the burly man at the back. He was wearing a heavy blacksmith's apron and going through some crates under the counter.

"Mr. Smithson, sir?"

"Yes?"

"Sorry to bother you, sir, but I'm looking for a man named Campbell. A horse trader, who I believe may be in town. Do you know him, sir?"

"'Course I do," the man answered in a deep, rumbling voice. He scratched at his massive barrel chest. "Just sold him some horses yesterday, as a matter of fact."

My heart beat a sure enough joyful song in my chest.

"Can you tell me where he's staying, sir? Where I could find him?"

"Well, he done left town."

Mr. Smithson must've seen my face fall 'cause he went on encouragingly, "But only just this morning, son. I had breakfast with him. He's heading over Walla Walla way. Probably didn't leave more than, say, an hour ago."

An hour! In all my travels and troubles, an hour was the closest I'd gotten to my Sarah. My breaths came fast and eager, like I was already running after her.

"Does he have his horses with him?"

"'Course he does. Nice big string, too, probably fifty head. He can't be moving too fast, neither. If you hurry on down the road toward Walla Walla, I reckon you could catch him soon enough. Can't miss him. He's got all those horses, and three or four men with him, and a covered wagon, too."

"Thank you, sir!" I said, already turning and running for the door.

Outside I turned to Ah-Kee and grabbed him by the shoulders. My voice was all shaky and high.

"We can catch her, Ah-Kee! Today! I hope you got some go left in your legs, 'cause we're gonna sure enough be *running*. You ready, Ah-Kee?"

Ah-Kee had been looking intently into my eyes, no doubt trying to figure out what I was hollering in his face, when suddenly his gaze went over my shoulder to something behind me. He gasped right out loud and stepped past me.

He shouted a word in Chinese. Then again. His voice, if it was possible, sounded even more excited than my own.

I turned, and I saw them.

A group of Chinese, probably ten or fifteen. They were walking up the road, holding bundles and bags. They had a couple mules with them, too, loaded down heavy.

They looked up when Ah-Kee called, and one of them stopped in his tracks. He took a step away from the group, toward me and Ah-Kee. He dropped the load he'd been carrying, right there in the mud of the street. His mouth hung wide open in clear surprise.

"Ah-Kee?" he said in a gaspy whisper. Then he shouted, like a man finally finding gold in his pan, "Ah-Kee! Ah-Kee!"

Ah-Kee left my side and ran across the muddy road and jumped right into that man's arms.

CHAPTER
17

There was an awful lot of hugging and crying and fast Chinese talking there in that muddy Yakima street. I stood in the rain by myself and watched.

The Chinese folks put down their bundles and bags, and they crowded around Ah-Kee and the man he'd run to. There were questions and answers and a whole bunch of fuss. After a few minutes, Ah-Kee turned and called me over with a shout and a wave. "Joseph! Joseph!" There was a kind of happy that I hadn't heard before in his voice.

I walked over through the mud, kinda shy, all those Chinese faces looking at me.

Another Chinese man, the tallest of them, stepped forward and exchanged a few words with Ah-Kee in Chinese. Then he turned to me. I was surprised when he started talking to me in broken but clear enough English.

"Ah-Kee say you have much travel together."

I nodded. "Yes, sir. We've traveled a good piece, me and Ah-Kee."

"He say you save him. He alone, you brought him here with you. We all very thanking you."

"Well, I was alone, too," I answered. "We brought each other, I reckon."

I cleared my throat and watched Ah-Kee with the man he'd run to. They were hugging tight like they weren't never gonna let go. Then Ah-Kee pulled away and reached into his pocket. He pulled out that little black stone bird sculpture and held it out. And that man, standing right there in that muddy street, reached in his own pocket and pulled out an exact match. A little carving, just like the one I'd seen Ah-Kee pull out and show to folks—and bears—for more miles than I cared to count. Ah-Kee and that man stood there in the rain and held those two birds close together, a matched set reunited.

And then I knew.

I'd already known that Ah-Kee was not just along for the ride, all those miles. He had been on a mission, too, just like I was. And right then I knew that what Ah-Kee had been looking for all along was even more important than a horse.

"That fella there," I said to the tall man next to me. My voice was kind of tight and scratchy. "That's Ah-Kee's papa, isn't it?"

"Yes," he answered. "He looking long time for son."

I nodded and sniffed.

"Yes, sir. I'm sure he was. And his son was looking for him, too."

Ah-Kee and his father walked over to me.

I put out my hand toward Ah-Kee's papa and he shook it, then bowed to me.

"We traveling now to Seattle," the tall man continued. "Many jobs there. Many Chinese."

"Oh." I pointed down the road toward Walla Walla, the one we were gonna run down to catch my Sarah. "Me and Ah-Kee are headed—" And then I stopped. 'Cause it hit me like a horse kick in my chest.

Ah-Kee wouldn't be coming with me.

Of course not. Against all the odds in heaven and earth, right here we'd stumbled smack into his people. He was back with his family. His folks. That's who Ah-Kee was meant to be with. Not some orphaned kid chasing a horse. It was clear as everything, but it took my breath right away. I stood there with my words stuck fast in my throat.

Ah-Kee slipped from his papa's arm and stepped toward me. He asked me a question, his voice steady and low and calm, like he was talking to a mama grizzly or birthing a baby. But his eyes were full of tears.

"Ah-Kee ask you if . . ." The tall man paused, finding the words. "He ask you if you need him. If you need him come with you."

Tears, hot and stinging, came to my eyes.

Ah-Kee was willing to leave his family. To be without his people again, in a foreign land, just to stay by my side and help me. I blinked and looked away, embarrassed with all them grown men looking at me. But I knew the tears wouldn't be blinked away. The thing to do was hold my head up and get it done.

"No, Ah-Kee," I said, shaking my head and keeping my voice firm as I could so my answer wouldn't need no translating. "No. You need to go. With your family. You need to be with your family."

Ah-Kee sniffled and nodded. He spoke a few more words.

"Ah-Kee say you good friend."

"He's a good friend, too. A real good friend."

The tears were sure enough coming, now, and I didn't try to hold them back. Ah-Kee talked, and the man translated.

"He say you, you . . . you honor. You honor your mother and father."

I swallowed a hard lump of hurting in my throat.

"I hope so. You tell Ah-Kee that he does, too."

The words were exchanged, and then Ah-Kee stepped right up to me. He reached in his pocket and pulled out the little black bird. The special stone memory he'd been carrying with him all along. The memory of his father. He pressed it into my hands.

I started to shake my head, but his hands were strong and sure. He closed my fingers tight around the carving and nodded once, looking in his serious way into my eyes.

I reached into my own pocket and pulled out the white stone from Papa's grave. I pressed it into Ah-Kee's hands, just like he'd pressed the bird into mine.

We looked at each other a minute, then we both put the other's memory into our own pocket. They were new memories, now, but they were tied up and bound to the old. That's how memories work, I suppose; you just go through life collecting them, never letting go of the precious ones but leaving room in your heart for more.

I shook Ah-Kee's hand, and we bowed to each other.

The rain picked up, working up toward a full-out shower. Puddles started pooling in the mud around us. My hair slicked down wet to my forehead. My voice was choked up, but I got my next words out.

"Good-bye, Ah-Kee. It's been a pleasure."

Ah-Kee stepped back to his papa, and I took a backward step in the direction I was going.

Then Ah-Kee asked one more thing, and the tall man passed it on.

"What is it you looking for?"

I almost laughed. All this way, all this struggle, and poor Ah-Kee hadn't even known what it was we were chasing after.

"A horse," I said. "My horse."

Ah-Kee cocked his head curious when the man gave him the answer.

"It was my family's horse. My papa gave it to me. My mama and my sister loved it. I'm the only one left. I got to get it back."

The man listened close, then passed my words on to Ah-Kee in Chinese.

Ah-Kee's eyebrows rose as he listened. His mouth wrinkled down in a frown. Then he nodded at me and spoke, just a few words.

"He hope you find it. He think you will."

"Thank you," I told Ah-Kee.

Ah-Kee spoke again. The man repeated the words in Chinese, a question in his voice, and Ah-Kee nodded and gestured for him to tell me.

"Ah-Kee say . . . he say for you to keep your pants on."

I laughed. A real, honest laugh, and wiped at my cheeks with a sleeve.

"All right. You tell him to work on his horse riding."

Ah-Kee laughed. And then we both walked away. In different directions.

I looked back once, just as he did. The group of Chinese was walking again, their backs bent under the loads they carried. Ah-Kee was already carrying a bundle, too. He raised his hand in a wave.

I waved back, through the rain that was now pouring down, soaking me to the skin.

Then I walked away, through the dripping mud, all alone in the world.

"It's just me and you again, Sarah," I whispered. "I'm coming for you."

*   *   *

My boots squished and squelched in the mud of the road. I left the last real buildings of Yakima behind and was soon passing the outskirts, just little shacks and houses here and there, and the railroad track off to one side. My going got slower and slower as the rain kept falling. The mud got deeper and clung to my boots and sucked at my feet, and soon every step was an effort. I was breathing hard and my heart was racing, and I wasn't hardly getting nowhere for it.

For the third time that day, I felt tears come to my eyes. I fought to hold them in. But it ain't a battle I won. My face was already wet with rain, and my tears mixed with it and were lost in the world. I didn't even know what kind of tears they were—tears of sadness, or of anger, or loneliness, or frustration. Most likely a bitter mix of all of them. But I couldn't hardly see through them. I was working my way up a hill but I was floundering in the slick and sticky mud, slipping back a step for every two I took. Finally my feet slid out from under me and I fell flat down in the mud, covering my shirt and pants, my hands buried to the wrists.

I pulled myself up to my knees but could go no farther. I knelt there in the mud, holding my tears.

I'd been a fool. A kid, wandering all over the countryside, looking for a horse he didn't even have the money to buy back. And what if I did finally catch up to Sarah, and did manage to get her back. What then? I had no home, no family. No folks or place to call my own. I'd have no stable to put her in, no hay to feed her. I was sure enough alone in the world. Having that horse back, as much as I loved her, wouldn't change that. Mama and Papa and Katie had left me behind. Even Ah-Kee was gone now. All that loneliness swirled around me and held me down like a giant, cold thumb.

But life is a funny thing. It just keeps on going on.

After a few minutes of kneeling there in the muck, my breathing calmed down. The rain let up a bit, winding down to just a slow, cold drizzle. A bird fluttered up, as alone as I was. He landed on the side of the road, ten or fifteen feet up, hopping and eyeing the ground sideways. Then he struck and pulled up a fat, slimy worm and flew off.

I looked around. Off in the distance, the Yakima River wound its curvy way through the valley. It made no sound from that far away, so I couldn't hear whatever story it was telling. Behind me, a steam locomotive was pulling out of Yakima, chugging and hissing, black clouds of coal smoke billowing out of its smokestack. It was heading toward me, on the tracks running just off to the side of the road.

A thought struck me, crouching there with soggy knees. I was alone, all right. And life had surely been a hard trial for me, so far. From the time Mama and Katie fell sick, life had been one misery after the other.

But here I was. Still with breath in my lungs. And blood in my veins. And memories and voices in my heart. Good ones. And life was going on, all around me. With or without me, it was going on.

It weren't a matter of the whole thing stopping or the whole thing going on. The whole thing was going on. It was only a matter of me standing up and deciding what part I had to play in it all.

I could be the quitting kind. Or not. I could be the kind of man my mama and papa had raised, or not.

I rose to my feet and did the best I could to scrape the worst of the mud off my coat and pants.

"Sarah is gonna be someone's horse," I said to myself. "And I'm sure as hell gonna make sure she's mine."

I took my first bold step forward and almost went right back to the ground again. In all my newfound vigor, I'd forgotten the mud. I was ready to move bravely on, but the mud had other ideas.

The train whistle blew behind me.

An idea leaped in my head like a fly-hungry trout.

I looked back at the train, moving slow but picking up speed. About a quarter mile behind me.

I swore at the mud and ran as best I could, up to the top of the rise that had been giving me such fits. Panting at the top, I squinted into the rain-blurred distance.

As far as I could see, the railroad tracks ran parallel to the road. Just right alongside it, more or less. All the way off into the distance.

Glancing back, I saw the train was closer and getting some good speed behind her. She'd be even with me in no time. I chewed on my cheek, trying to decide.

Hopping a train was a crime. If a railroad man saw you hopping on without a paid ticket, you'd likely feel the blow of an ax handle. You could get thrown in jail, even, if they caught you.

But my options were running out. I was only a couple hours back from Sarah now. The mud had to be slowing them down near as much as it did me. Once the rain cleared, though, there'd be no keeping up. This was likely my last and only chance to catch her. She was heading east, forever away; but she was here now, by God, and I was alive enough still to die trying to get her back.

I ran off the road and into the brush. There was a bushy Russian olive tree just back from the tracks, and I crouched down quick behind it. Those twin steel rails were humming and rattling, telling me about the train coming my way.

I slipped Ah-Kee's little bird out of my pocket and into the satchel, making sure it was buckled shut and snug around my shoulder. Inside was a gun, and some money, and the memory of a friend; I didn't intend to lose any of it. I threw Ezra Bishop's whip off into the bushes to lighten my load. I hoped nobody ever found the cursed thing—but if they did, I prayed they used it for saving drowning people and not for whipping horses.

I crouched in the drizzling rain, waiting for that train to appear, and I thought about Sarah. I thought about how sometimes, if it was early-morning dark and I whistled for her across the pasture, all I'd hear was her hooves galloping toward me; at first I'd see only her white splotches in the blackness, and then she'd be right up against me, bumping me with her chest and nuzzling at my neck with the warm softness of her nose.

I wasn't thinking about the rain or the road or the loneliness. I was thinking about things we lose, and things we have to hold on to, and things we have to fight to get back.

I wiped my hands as dry as I could on any part of my clothes I could find that weren't covered in mud. I started to say a little prayer—either to Mama or to the Lord, I wasn't sure—but the sound of the oncoming train grew to a roar, pushing all the words outta my head.

Then it went past, in a lung-sucking gust of wind and an ear-punching thunder that shook the teeth in my jaw. I gritted my teeth and screwed my eyes shut, willing my heart to hold tight to its courage and not let that train shake it loose.

But I couldn't keep my eyes closed for long. The train was almost going faster now than I could run. If it got past me, I wouldn't catch it.

I peeked over the bush. The caboose was only five cars away. But right before the caboose was a freight car. A freight car with a metal ladder bolted to its side.

I licked my lips and flexed my legs and crouched, ready to run. I waited, breathless.

Three. Two. One.

I took off, running alongside the train, my feet pounding the gravel of the railbed. The train kept speeding past me, but with every stride I took, I got closer to matching its speed. When we were almost even and the train was just barely crawling past me, I looked up.

The ladder was about ten feet behind me, and coming up. My legs churned and my lungs gulped air hungrily.

I looked quickly forward, and almost stumbled to a stop. Right ahead of me and coming fast was a timber post, with a sign on it . . . some sort of train signal for the engineer. It was right in my path. There was no time for thinking.

I jumped.

Up, and back, and to the side. To catch that ladder as it went rushing past.

There it was. My hand stretched. I felt the metal of the ladder slap my palm and my fingers closed tight like a trap on a beaver. My foot reached up and found a rung. But I felt myself swinging out, away from the train, twisting backwards through the air as I held on with only one hand and one foot. I knew that signal post was coming up, that it was gonna smack me like the hand of God and cave my skull in.

With a desperate scream I pulled myself in, my muscles straining, tight up against the train, grabbing that blessed ladder with both hands. I felt the signal post whistle past me, kissing at the coat on my back but leaving me be.

I clung to the ladder, breathing like a drowning man pulled from the ocean.

I was moving now, and fast.

The world was moving on, all right, but I was moving with it. And in just the direction I needed to go.

CHAPTER
18

The ground sped by under my feet, zipping by so fast it made my stomach turn and I had to close my eyes to keep from losing my breakfast. I held on as tight as my fingers could grip, got both feet firm on the rungs, and then hugged that ladder like it was my mama.

Once I caught my breath, I relaxed a bit. Just enough to open my eyes and look out ahead. I could still see the road, off to the side, a muddy track cutting through the countryside. I knew I had to keep my eye on it. I couldn't let myself fly right past Mr. Campbell and my horse.

A smile broke through my fear. The world was sure enough *flying* under me. Faster than I could walk. Faster than I could run. Faster than a *horse* could run, at least in that mud. I was getting closer and closer at last to my Sarah.

I knew I had miles to go yet, but I kept my eyes trained on that road. Sometimes it ran off dangerously far from the train tracks, barely visible off in the distance, but I knew if I kept my eyes sharp I wouldn't be able to miss fifty horses and a covered wagon.

Seconds ticked by, then minutes. Then, likely an hour. My fear turned to excitement, then to boredom, then to nervousness. Had I missed them somehow? Were they on a different road? My stomach knotted with worry. Going fast is mighty fine, but going fast in the wrong direction is worse than not going anywhere at all.

Eventually even my nervousness gave way to a dangerous exhaustion. My fingers and arms cramped and burned, and

I had to shift from side to side to keep from losing my grip. My back was aching, and the thin metal rung of the ladder stabbed into the bottoms of my feet like a drill.

I was bending down low, stretching and flexing my aching leg muscles, when I saw him. A man, on the road. Running his horse just as fast as he could, back toward Yakima. I straightened up quick and eyed him. He looked scared. A little desperate, maybe. He was slapping his horse with his hat and going a heckuva lot quicker than was probably safe in all that mud. I swallowed grimly. There ain't no good reason for a man to be racing down a muddy road in the rain all scared like that. And whatever he was running from I was heading toward, and my Sarah was already there.

I quit with my bending and shifting, ignoring the protests of my body. I stood straight and I watched that road.

Then I saw it. Under the gray sky in all that bare country, it was unmistakable. The rounded white top of a covered wagon. I held my breath and stretched up to my tippy-toes. There was a stirring crowd around it, and as I got closer the crowd became horses. Plenty of 'em. And some paints among them, too. My breath came back, fast.

Mr. Campbell. And Sarah. My Sarah, at last.

I loosed my grip a bit and leaned back, getting ready to jump. But that train was sure enough moving fast, even faster than when I'd jumped on. Getting off now would be like jumping off a horse at an all-out sprint, with nothing but the rocky ground to catch you.

But it had to be done. So there was nothing to do but to do it. I sure as heck wasn't gonna ride that train right past my Sarah.

I peered ahead through the falling rain and saw a big bush coming up. Just close enough to the tracks, maybe, if I pushed off real good. It wouldn't be soft, necessarily, but it'd sure as heck be softer than all the rocks that were my only other option.

One thing I didn't have was much time to make up my mind.

The bush came rushing up. I crouched, legs tight and ready for the spring. I let go of the ladder with one hand and leaned back into the rushing air.

For a split second I thought of Ah-Kee, and wished he was jumping with me.

Then the bush was there and I fired both legs like loaded pistols and let go of the ladder.

I flew through the air like a shot arrow. The bush came rushing at me faster than I was expecting. I just had time to close my eyes and cover my face with my arms. Then there was a crash and a tangle and a thousand scratches and then a thud and I was on the ground, breathless and bruised, with a mouthful of leaves.

I ain't sure how the leaves got in my mouth. Must've had it open, I s'pose. I was probably screaming, but too scared to notice. I shook my head and spit 'em out.

I gave my body a good once-over, shaking my limbs and wiggling my toes and fingers, then got gingerly up to my feet. Everything seemed in order, though a little sore and touchy in places.

I wiped a little blood off a scratch across my forehead and took off at a jog toward that covered wagon and my horse.

My heart was getting ready to start singing. I had that early morning Christmas feeling rattling around in my insides. I was gonna see my Sarah again, gonna scratch her neck and look into those warm brown eyes at last.

But when I broke out of the brush onto the muddy road, about twenty feet from the wagon, I could tell right off that something was wrong. Terribly wrong.

The wagon weren't moving. The horses were high-stepping and tossing their heads, all nervous-like. They were tied up together in bunches all around and behind the wagon. I couldn't see right off if Sarah was among 'em.

But I could see the men, gathered and crouched around something lying in the mud of the road.

It was a body. And it weren't moving, neither.

The men had their hats off.

I stopped my running and walked up, slow and easy.

There were three men still breathing, two standing up and one kneeling down by the body. They turned to look as I walked up to 'em. The rain pattered down all around us.

They all had mournful faces. None of 'em spoke.

"What happened?" I asked.

"That damned dirty Caleb Fawney," one of the men answered, his voice scratchy and low. "That's what."

My blood ran a heart-chilling kind of cold. I'd heard the name Caleb Fawney before. He was a known outlaw, wanted for some time in these parts. There was a bounty on his head. He'd killed eleven men, I'd heard. I looked at the body in the road. I reckoned he was number twelve.

The corpse belonged to a young man, no more than twenty, with a clean-shaven face and a cleft in his chin. His eyes were open, staring empty up at the sky that was sprinkling his dead face with rain. A gun lay limp in one outstretched hand.

"He was waiting for us," the man went on. "He took our money, and our guns." The man sighed and spit onto the ground. "Then Travis here went for his gun, the fool. Mr. Fawney shot him down without so much as blinking. Then he took the fastest horse off our string and took off up that trail there. We sent James to run back to Yakima and fetch up a posse, but Mr. Fawney'll be long gone by the time they get here."

I was still staring shocked at that dead man when the words broke through my fog.

"He took your fastest horse?" My eyes scanned the horses quick. There were all kinds, paints and bays and blacks. But I didn't see a red-and-white Indian pony with a notched ear among them. "A red-and-white paint? That you bought from Ezra Bishop?"

The man cocked his head at me.

"How'd you figure that, son?"

"Are you Mr. Campbell?"

"Yeah," he answered cautiously.

"My name is Joseph Johnson, sir. That horse is mine, unlawfully bought by Mr. Bishop. I've been trailing her for more miles than I care to figure. I've come all the way from Old Mission in the Wenatchee Valley to get that horse back."

"Well, son, I hate to disappoint you. But looks like your adventure ends here. Your horse is with Caleb Fawney now. It's the end of the road for you."

I wiped the rain out of my eyes with a soggy sleeve.

"No, sir," I answered him. "It is not. My road ends when I have that horse back. Not a muddy foot sooner." I looked over the horses milling nervously about. "Could I borrow one of your horses, sir?"

"Borrow one of my . . ." Mr. Campbell's voice trailed off, mystified.

"Yes, sir. I aim to catch up to Mr. Fawney and retrieve my horse. And maybe get your money back, too. But I'll need a good quick mount, and now."

"Son, now hold on. You can't go charging after a man like Caleb Fawney unarmed. Why do you think we're all standing here?"

I pulled Papa's pistol out of the satchel and held it up, pointed at the sky.

"I ain't unarmed, sir. And I am going after him, no matter what. I'd rather not go on foot, and I'd sure be obliged if you'd lend me a horse."

He took a few steps forward, hands outstretched to reason with me.

"Now, son, I appreciate what you're saying and all but . . ." And then Mr. Campbell got close enough to look in my eyes. He stopped short, his face thoughtful.

"By God," he said. "You *are* going after him, ain't you?"

"Yes, sir."

Mr. Campbell scratched his neck and looked around, then back at me.

"Listen, the law and the ladies will never let me be if I let a boy go after the likes of Caleb Fawney. Point your gun at me, son."

"Pardon?"

"Go ahead. Point your gun at me." I saw an earnestness in Mr. Campbell's eyes, so I reluctantly lowered the gun 'til its barrel was pointed more or less in Mr. Campbell's general direction.

He raised both hands in the air.

"Holy blazes, boys, he's got me beat. I s'pose I have no choice. I cannot leave my children orphans, if I ever have any. Yes, son, you can take one of my horses. I'd recommend that gray stallion over there, already saddled. He's fast and steady and good in the mud."

I smiled.

"Thank you, sir. I'll bring him back, riding my own."

"I hope so."

I was on the stallion and ready to give him my heels when Mr. Campbell called out to me.

"You keep your guard up, Joseph Johnson. Caleb Fawney is bad all the way through. He will not think twice before putting a bullet in you. He will not bluff, and he will not hesitate. You best do the same."

I nodded, the stallion stomping the dirt beneath me. I held the reins in one hand, Papa's pistol in the other.

"Yes, sir. This here has got to be done. And I do intend to do it."

The trail Mr. Campbell had pointed out took off straight up a slope from the road. I held the reins in my mouth so I could grip the saddle horn tight, and gave that stallion a good kick. He was a fine horse, all right, and he charged right up the hill.

At the top I could see the trail winding ahead through the sagebrush, flat and level for a ways, before dropping down and out of sight into a draw. I slowed for a few paces, just long enough to double-check I had a bullet in the chamber and to put the reins back into my other hand. Then I slapped those reins down on that stallion's neck and kicked with both heels and we were off, racing after the outlaw and murderer who had stolen my horse.

We sprinted through the rain, mud flying up from under the stallion's hooves. I had to wipe with my sleeve to keep from getting blinded by the falling rain. But my teeth were set hard, and all the determination in my heart left no real room for fear.

I sharpened my eyes and readied my shooting hand as we dropped down into the draw, but the trail ahead stayed empty. Up the draw we ran, the sound of our beating hooves and panting lungs lost in all the rain.

Dark clouds by now had blocked out nearly all the sun, and a heavy mist hung in the chilled air. Between the clouds and the rain and the mist it was sure enough dark, looking closer to dusk than noon. I squinted ahead, ready to see my horse and the man upon her.

The trail ran straight up the draw, which was choked with brush and trees. The walls of the little canyon were close, and low. I could've thrown a rock from one side to the other, or from the bottom to the top. It was a tight place, dark and cramped, and not the kind of place at all that I wanted to come upon an armed outlaw.

"I'm coming for you, Sarah," I panted in time with the stallion's running. "I'm coming for—"

And just right then we came 'round a corner, and there they were.

Caleb Fawney, down on his knees, digging in the dirt underneath a tree.

And, tied off to the tree next to him, ears pricked up and eyes on me and that stallion coming 'round the bend, was my horse. My sweet Sarah, her red and white showing bright in the dim grayness. My horse.

My heart swelled and sung and nearly beat to bursting, and all I wanted to do was jump off that stallion and toss down my gun and run to her and throw my arms around her neck and bury my nose in her mane and just cry out all my sadness into her warm fur.

But my head knew better than my heart; it knew there was something to be done, and I was the only one to do it.

Caleb Fawney's face snapped toward me and he jumped to his feet. But before his murderer's hands could move an inch toward the guns on his waist I hollered out, "Stop! Hands up! You reach for those guns and you're a dead man!" And my voice had no little boy waver in it, no shake or squeak. My voice was as strong as the stallion beneath me, and as sure and solid as the pistol in my hand.

And Caleb Fawney froze. There was a breathless heart-beat of time, there in the rain, when he stood deciding what to do. I reined the stallion to a halt and sat upon him, looking down the barrel of my gun at a man I was fully prepared to kill if I needed to.

CHAPTER
19

Slowly, Caleb Fawney raised his hands in the air above his head.

"Keep 'em there," I said. Without blinking or looking away once I slid down off the horse, keeping my gun on him all the while. Once on the ground, I took a few careful steps toward him. He narrowed his eyes at me, then his mouth dropped open.

"Aw, hell, you're just a boy!" he exclaimed, and I saw his body relax.

"I'm a boy with a gun," I warned him. "And this trigger don't care the age of the finger that pulls it. Don't test me, sir. I will shoot."

At the sound of my voice Sarah let out a loud whinny and strained against her rope, kicking her feet at the ground. I held my heart in check and kept my eyes on a man I knew I couldn't trust.

"What kind of a posse are you?" he asked me. "Is this what they send after outlaws 'round here?"

"I ain't after no outlaw," I said. "I'm after my horse, and you've got her."

Caleb Fawney looked over at Sarah.

"What, this pony here? You're here for the horse?"

"Yes, sir. She rightfully belongs to me, and I'm here to get her back." I paused. I didn't want to get too close to the outlaw. "Untie her, please, and send her over."

"Why in the world should I give you my horse?"

I gritted my teeth.

"She ain't your horse. And this gun pointed at your chest ought to be reason enough, I reckon."

Caleb Fawney licked his lips.

"Where'd you get that gun, kid? Whose is it?" I didn't like the fake easy tone of his voice. Like he was biding his time, waiting for his moment.

I looked him right in his outlaw eyes, my voice hard as a hammer.

"This here was my papa's pistol," I said. "But it's mine, now. And I'll shoot you dead if you go for your guns, sir."

"All right, all right," Caleb Fawney said, shaking his hands in the air. "You got me beat, kid. But I still don't see why I gotta give you this horse here when you've already got a fine one there."

"That horse there," I answered, "is my horse. She is my horse. She was given to me by my papa, who taught me to ride her when I could hardly walk myself. That horse there carried my mama when she was too pregnant with my sister to walk on her own. That horse there is the horse I gave my little sister rides on, to teach her not to be afraid. My papa always said it was my duty to take care of her, and that is what I am doing."

The man smiled at me, a smile I sure enough didn't like one bit.

"That's an awful big job for a boy, chasing down a known murderer all by yourself. Where's your pa? And your ma?"

"My papa died, crushed by a rolling wagon. Mama passed on first, from typhoid, along with my little sister. It's just me, now. Just me and that horse. She's the only bit of my family I got left, sir." My voice trailed off. I looked away and sniffed, then real quick brought my eyes back to him. "She's the only bit of *me* I got left."

Caleb Fawney's smile faded as I spoke.

"So you're an orphan, then."

"No, sir."

"Well, you ain't got no family, do you?"

"I do have a family, sir. They're just all dead. But they're my family just the same. So I ain't no orphan. I'm still my mama's son and my papa's boy and my sister's brother, and I'm here to get our horse back."

For a moment, there was only the sound of the rain and Sarah's stamping, as she pulled on the rope trying to get to me.

Then the outlaw spoke.

"Fine, kid. She's yours. Take it easy, now. I'm gonna have to move to untie her."

My hand shook not a bit as the gun barrel followed Caleb Fawney over to my Sarah. He kept his eyes on me, and he moved nice and slow. My finger stayed tight on the trigger, ready in an instant to squeeze until death came out.

Caleb Fawney sidestepped to Sarah. He bent down and with one hand reached for her bridle, tied off to a low branch. His fingers unworked the knot easily, and he slid the leather loose from the limb. With a quick flick of his wrist he released her, the rope falling slack.

Sarah tossed her head and, feeling her freedom, she ran toward me.

Fighting every urge I had in me to run to her, too, I stepped quick to the side so that she didn't place herself between me and the outlaw. His eyes were speedy, watching me, watching my gun, watching my horse. I knew that he was a rattlesnake with no rattle, coiled quiet and waiting for the time to strike.

And then Sarah was there, right there with me. My Sarah, my sweet, lost Sarah, was sure enough right there with me again, right there up against me. Her nose nuzzled hard at my neck, nearly pushing me down, knocking me so that I had to step to stay up. She butted her chest up against my shoulder, rubbing her neck against my head. My Sarah, my sweet, lost Sarah, was sure enough right there with me again. And I was with her. I was back with my horse, my girl.

My eyes got dangerously blurry with tears. I blinked them away furiously, keeping my eyes on Caleb Fawney, keeping that gun steady on his heart. Sarah bumped and nuzzled me, her sweet breath blowing in my ears and on my neck. I wrapped my other arm up around her neck and hugged her tight, and she rested her head down across my shoulders, and every broken piece of me came together right there in that one sure enough beautiful moment.

"Good Lord," Caleb Fawney said, his voice not much more than a whisper. "That horse sure does love you, don't she?"

I didn't answer, not trusting my voice to talk.

"Well, okay," he finally said. "Send that stallion on over, then, and let's go our separate ways. I ain't in any position to spend any more time standing around talking."

I took a bracing breath, knowing that my next words would bring only trouble and danger. I kept my arm 'round my horse and my gun dead level.

"No, sir. This stallion ain't my horse to give."

Caleb Fawney's eyebrows dropped. I saw all the casual drop out of his shoulders. His fingers flexed and loosened, ready. A deadly calm fell over his face.

"Excuse me? You telling me you aim to leave me on foot, with a posse no doubt on its way here right now? After I done already gave you what you came for?"

"No, sir." I kept my finger tight, my eyes hard and wide. "I don't intend to leave you at all. There is an innocent man back there, murdered in the mud. And my papa taught me to always do the right thing, even when it's hard."

Caleb Fawney just stared at me, still and silent, eyes unblinking. My heart was a-hammering.

I pointed with my chin at the hole he'd been digging when I'd rode up. Sitting in it was a sack. Mr. Campbell's money, I was sure.

"Grab that bag, please, sir. Nice and easy. That is stolen money, and I aim to return it to its rightful owner."

Caleb Fawney blinked a slow, lazy blink. I didn't like the kind of calm that he was becoming. Like this was the kind of situation he was used to, and good at. And I was not. Like he was the snake, and I was the mouse.

"Now, boy, you know that ain't gonna happen." His voice was cold like January snow down my collar. "Going back with you means me hanging from a tree. I don't intend for that to happen." He took a few careful steps to the side, edging away so that Sarah was more between him and me.

"You'll get a fair trial," I said, begging him in my heart to not make this happen like I thought it was gonna happen. I circled with him, trying to keep my shot clear.

"Maybe," he said. "But we both know a fair trial still ends with a rope around my neck. Put down your gun, kid. I don't wanna hurt you."

"I don't wanna hurt you neither, sir. Keep your hands up. And stop moving!"

The rain was back to pouring. It pittered on the leaves around us. It ran down my face and into my eyes. But I didn't dare wipe at them with my sleeve. That moment was all that Caleb Fawney would need to draw his gun and put a bullet in me. His own eyes were dry and cold under the brim of his hat.

"Me and you are a lot alike," he said, taking another step to the side. I stepped with him, almost tripping on a root but keeping my footing. "I was an orphan, too, you know. But my papa never taught me nothing but drinkin' and meanness."

"You stop that walkin' right now!"

Caleb Fawney ignored me, moving again to the side, forcing me to take another stumbling step to keep him in my sights and Sarah in the clear.

"But he also taught me that a man ought to know when it's time for him to go," he said.

And then I saw it.

I saw it in his eyes, the way they sharpened and widened.

I saw it in his breathing, how it sped up and then stopped, waiting.

I saw it in his whole body, the way it just barely tightened up, just barely got smaller and harder like a spring shaking to be sprung.

It was all small, but it was all there. I knew, in one terrible moment, that the outlaw Caleb Fawney was about to go for his gun.

"No!" I started to shout, wanting anything at all except to pull the trigger.

But Caleb Fawney's hand shot like dark lightning toward the gun at his hip.

I waited just a blink of a breath of a heartbeat of a moment, wordlessly praying that it wasn't all happening.

And then I saw his hand coming up with a shiny black pistol.

And I sure enough pulled that heartless trigger.

And Papa's gun roared and kicked in my shaking hand.

CHAPTER
20

Everything stood terribly still when that gun in my hand went off.

My breathing.

My pounding heart.

Even the rain, I think, stopped its falling for just a moment.

Caleb Fawney stood there, looking at me, the gun in his hand. It was halfway up, pointing at the ground somewhere in front of my feet.

He blinked at me. And a queer sort of smile played on his lips.

I missed him! I thought, and I wasn't disappointed. I was darned near relieved that my bullet had missed its mark, and that Caleb Fawney was still standing there in front of me.

And then he crumpled to the ground, landing on his back in the mud.

I stood there. The rain started up again. My lungs took a shaky breath. My heart started my blood moving again.

Caleb Fawney, staring up at the clouds, heaved a big sigh. He'd dropped his gun on the way down and had landed so that his head was resting on a log. His hat was still on, even. It looked almost like he was just lying down for a nap.

I walked over to him, slow. My stomach twisted with a sour sickness. Just to be safe, I kicked his gun back behind me as I approached. I kept my pistol pointed at him, though it sure didn't hardly seem necessary.

I stood looking down at him, my heart up in my throat.

"Damn it, kid," he said through a clenched jaw. "You shot me."

He was clutching at his stomach with both hands and I could see the dark spreading blood stain, right in his middle, just under his heart. The gun shook wildly in my hand. I fought to keep from getting sick.

"I'm sorry," I said. And my voice was back to being shaky and high again. I weren't no man at all, and I knew it. I was just a boy. A boy who had just shot a man.

He closed his eyes and his face tightened up in a grimace. He bared his teeth like a wolf caught in the jaws of a steel trap. Then he groaned, and took a few breaths, and opened his eyes into slits and looked at me.

"Get on outta here," he snarled through a tight breath. He was talking like he was carrying something mighty heavy, something he couldn't carry for too much longer. "Get on outta here and let me die in peace."

"I—I—I'll come back," I said. "With a doctor." My breath was coming in quick, shaking gasps, like I'd just run a race.

He shook his head once, quick, and coughed out a hurting laugh.

"I'm dead, kid. Gut shot. It's just a matter of bleeding out, now."

Rain poured down on us, drenching us both in the same wetness.

"I don't wanna just leave you," I said. "All alone."

He shook his head again.

"I always been alone. Go on and leave. I don't wanna die with someone gawking at me."

I shifted from foot to foot, the rain running down my face and down my back.

"Before you go . . . could you . . . do me a favor?" His voice was getting smaller, and tighter. His words were getting shorter. I could tell each one was an effort.

"Yes, sir."

"I got a flask. In my pocket. Let me get it out."

I tightened my grip on the gun.

"Okay," I said.

His hand, stained with blood, crawled up from his wound to his pocket. He fished out a dull pewter flask. His breathing was coming fast and shallow.

He held the flask out toward me, his hand weaving unsteadily.

"Open it, kid."

I stepped forward, real cautious, and took it from him. My gun stayed as steady on him as my trembling hand would allow. I unscrewed his flask and handed it back. He brought it to his lips with a quivering hand and took a long draw. Then he held it out to me again.

"Have a drink."

I swallowed.

"No, thank you, sir. I—I don't drink."

He winced and closed his eyes, then blew out a breath and opened them again.

"Take a drink. Ain't gonna hurt you none. I'll be dead shortly. I wanna have one last drink. And I don't feel like drinking alone."

Mama and Papa were silent on this one. They wouldn't have liked me drinking. But as Mama said, mercy and humanity were in short enough supply in this world.

I took the flask. It was sticky with his blood. It felt warm in my hand. I hesitated a moment, then tilted it back and took a swallow. It burned something fierce and I coughed and sputtered, but I didn't spit it out. My throat was on fire.

I gave him back the flask with a trembling hand.

"Now go on," he said. "Get on outta here and leave me in peace."

I took a step back and remembered his gun, lying a few paces behind me.

"I can't leave you your gun," I said.

"Why's that?" he grunted, fixing me with a one-eyed glare. "You gonna leave me here defenseless? With a posse coming after me?"

"Yes, sir. I'm sorry. But there's good men in that posse."

Caleb Fawney smiled a bitter, weary smile.

"You'd be surprised how bad a good man can look when he's coming to kill you."

"I s'pose so. But I can't leave you armed. Is there—is there anything I can do for you, sir? Before I go?"

"Nah. Just leave me be. I got some dying to do."

I took a few more steps back and picked up his gun and put it in my satchel.

Sarah came up behind me and nudged at the back of my neck with her nose. I reached up and scratched her cheek. My heart was a sure enough painful confusion, full of so much sad and happy at the same time.

I stepped back and buried my face in Sarah's mane for a few breaths, taking my eyes off of Caleb Fawney for just a moment. I breathed in her good, horse smell and wiped the tears off my face into her mane.

"Kid!" he called out. My head snapped up. I was sure I'd see him standing there, another gun in his hand. But he was still lying in the mud, limp and unmoving.

"You done right by killing me," he said. "It shouldn't weigh none on you. I was gonna shoot you. You beat me square, and you shot true. You done right. One of us was gonna die. And I reckon it may as well have been me."

He reached up and pulled the hat from his head. Then he threw it toward me. It spun and floated and landed in the dirt at my feet.

"Take that. It's a good hat. Shouldn't go to waste. Keep the rain off your face." His voice was getting weaker and more pained every second.

I looked down at the hat at my feet, then stooped and

picked it up. I put it on my head and looked over at Caleb Fawney. The rain pittered and pattered on the wide brim of the hat.

His chest was rising and falling, quick and ragged.

I ain't proud of it, but it's sure enough true: I didn't want to be there and have to watch him die. I didn't.

I walked around to my Sarah's side. All she had was a bridle around her neck. Mr. Fawney had been riding her bareback, just like I did. I had to look away from him and lower my gun to get up on her, but it didn't worry me none. I knew he was past hurting me.

With a grunt and a jump I was up, back where I belonged. Up on my Sarah's back, her mane clutched tight in my free hand. I felt her breathing and living between my legs. I looked at Mr. Fawney's blood, staining my left hand. Sarah felt good and familiar under me, but I didn't feel like a child no more. But I put the pistol back in my satchel all the same. 'Cause I'd sure enough had my fill of being a man, for a while.

The rain was coming down hard now. It drummed a steady beat on the hat on my head. The black clouds were gathered so dark it seemed almost like night.

"Mr. Fawney," I said. "For what it's worth, I don't think you're bad all the way through."

Caleb Fawney grimaced and grunted.

"Well, kid. Then that makes one of us. Now get the hell outta here."

I gave my Sarah a squeeze. It didn't take no kick or

nothing. We were like one, her and me. She turned without me telling her and took us right where I needed to go, back the way I'd come.

"That's my girl," I said, bending low and patting her on her strong neck. "That's my girl."

Mr. Campbell's horse, standing in all that wet, far from any person he knew, was more than willing to follow us back down that draw. His hooves rumbled behind us as we headed toward the road and the waiting world.

I did not look back at Caleb Fawney, dying in that rain from the bullet I put in him. I did not look back. I couldn't.

The cold mist was even thicker than it had been, shrouding the world in a gray fog that chilled through my clothes and brought gooseflesh out all over me.

My heart was all kinds of broken. I'd shot a man. I'd shot a man and left him for dead in the rain. My heart was all kinds of cold, and all kinds of scared, and all kinds of lonely.

So as we galloped through that murk, my heart started talking to Sarah. Though my mouth was closed, I started telling her all about my long road to find her. About Ah-Kee, and the last grizzly in the Colockum, and what was left of the Indians. About Ezra Bishop, who she knew, and almost drowning in the Yakima. About boys and babies and a cabin in a canyon. About saying good-bye to a friend, and riding a train through the rain. About a man lying dying in the mud, and a grown-up boy back on the horse he loved. And behind that story, we were telling each other another story we both knew. A story about a mama and a papa and a son and a sister. And a red-and-white Indian paint pony. A story about home, and a story about family.

We were right together, again and at last. Like we were always meant to be. Me and my sweet Sarah.

Mr. Fawney's hat kept the rain off my face, but my cheeks were wet nonetheless. My tears were like a river, and they were sure enough telling a story.

Once we'd come up out of the draw, back to the straight flat part of the trail that led to the road, Sarah felt my feet before I kicked them and we sped up, rising to a gallop through that open country. I let her loose, let her open up and run. I let her run as fast as she wanted, taking us both away from the blood I'd spilled and the man I'd sent to the grave.

The wind of our running was blowing on my face. I couldn't see far through the mist and the darkness and the rain, but I could see the horse beneath me and that was all I needed to see.

And then my Sarah jerked, hard. I felt her body shudder and heard a dull sound like she'd been slapped with a stick.

I felt us falling, plunging all of a sudden down from where we'd been flying, down toward the earth.

And just before I hit the dirt, just before I smashed into the hard and hateful ground, I heard the echoing crack of the gunshot.

As the mud rushed up toward me, I knew with a cold and sickening certainty. I knew.

I knew that she'd been shot.

My Sarah, my sweet Sarah, had been shot right out from under me.

CHAPTER
21

I lay stunned, the breath knocked clean out of my body and the sense knocked clean out of my head. My face was smashed down in the mud. I blinked and groaned and tried to gather my wits.

Then I heard Sarah. Behind me. When we fell I'd been thrown forward, over her head. She was breathing hard and kind of grunting with each breath. And I could tell by where her breathing was coming from that she was still down, still lying there on the ground. It ain't never good when a horse doesn't get up.

I jumped right up, ignoring the aches in my body. I stumbled back to where she lay on her side. Her eyes were open and rolling whitely. Her muscles twitched and jerked. I dropped to my knees beside her and threw my arms around her neck.

"Sarah!" I shouted. "Sarah!" Her great heart was pounding. Her rapid breaths blew out hard through her nostrils.

I felt a warm stickiness on my arm and sat back in the mud, letting her go.

The bullet had got her right in her neck. Right in the middle, between her shoulder and her head.

It was a wet, seeping wound, blood spilling out like struck oil. It matted in her mane and stained her white parts red.

"Oh, Sarah," I said through tears. Her breath was slowing down, gasp by gasp. I didn't like how her mouth hung open, how her tongue just flopped out in the mud. "Oh, Sarah, no."

She was my Sarah, my half-wild Indian pony. She was my memory, my family, my home. I'd gone all that way, all those miles, through all that hardship, to have her back with me where she belonged. And now I was losing her.

The hooves of running horses came upon us fast and fierce, but I didn't even look up. My eyes and my heart were locked steady on my horse, lying there suffering.

"Hands up!" a voice hollered, but I kept my hands soft on poor sweet Sarah. She needed to know I was there, with her. "Hands up!" the voice shouted again. Though I didn't raise my hands, I did finally raise my head and look up at the voice through hot tears.

"You shot my horse," I said, my voice broken. The man sat high on a black horse. He was holding a rifle pointed straight at me. He was tall and thin, with a big bushy salt-and-pepper mustache above his tight mouth and a shining silver star pinned to his chest. More men on horseback came up behind him and spread out to either side, guns drawn on me.

The man squinted at me through the dim light and falling rain, and his mouth slowly fell open. He lowered his gun and swore.

"It ain't Fawney," he said to the other men, who lowered their guns as well. "It's the boy. It's just the boy." He swore again.

"You shot my horse," I repeated.

The man looked down at Sarah, bleeding out in the mud.

"I'm sorry, son. You came charging up toward us.

Bareback on that red-and-white pony, wearing that hat. We thought you was Caleb Fawney."

He hopped down off his horse with a squeak of saddle leather and walked over to where I knelt. He looked down for a moment, then sighed and swore, and I heard him cock a round into his rifle's chamber.

"Step aside, son," he said.

I spun around. He held his gun ready, his finger on the trigger.

"What are you doing?" I demanded.

The man's face was grim, his eyes sorrowful.

"I'm putting yer horse out of her misery."

"No! You can't kill her!"

The man sighed a heavy sigh from the bottom of his lungs.

"I'm afraid I already did. She's suffering. Now go ahead and get on outta the way so I can end it."

"I won't let you! I won't let you shoot her!"

He looked into my eyes. His were dark and somber, but there weren't no meanness in them. They reminded me of Papa's, after Mama and Katie died.

"Listen. You ain't doing her no favors. She's shot through the neck. Look at the blood, boy. The only way to take care of her now is to let her go. That's what you gotta do. You gotta let her go. So the hurtin' can stop. It ain't a cruelty, son . . . it's a mercy."

I looked at him, my lungs heaving. My eyes wet and hot. Feeling so much. Remembering so much. Remembering

Papa and Mama, and Katie. I tried to feel them, tried to reach out with my heart and feel my parents and my sister. I tried to know what to do.

And I did. I knew. I sure enough knew. I knew how Papa would want me to take care of my horse, even if it was hard. Even if it was the hardest thing in the world. And I knew how Mama would always expect kindness from me above all else, even if it was painful. And I knew that Katie would never be able to stand seeing our sweet Sarah suffer.

I was soaked right through with rain. When I spoke, my teeth chattered.

"All right," I said, my voice a weak croak. "All right."

I turned back to my Sarah. Her breathing had calmed down to a weak, regular rhythm.

"Oh, girl," I said, choking. I ran my hands up her neck, scratched my fingers into her mane. "Oh, my sweet girl." I bent down, pressing my head against hers, pressing my chest against her neck. My tears flowed down onto her skin just like her blood flowed down onto the muddy ground.

It was all with me, there. All of it. My memories, my very earliest memories of riding her and loving her. My memories of her and me and Papa and Mama. And Katie. Katie, who adored her like nothing else. How gentle Sarah was, how sweet. But how strong and fast and stubborn, too. I thought of Ezra Bishop whipping her, because she wouldn't leave me behind.

"You are the best horse in the whole world," I whispered into her mane. "The very best." Her breathing was ragged and broken. I squeezed her neck in a hug, like I could hold her tight enough to keep her there with me, among the living. "I love you."

I was sure enough saying good-bye to that horse. I was squeezing her tight, but at the same time I was sure enough letting her go.

I thought of sunsets and leaves and how they're even more beautiful when they're dying.

Through my shirt, through the rain and her blood, I felt my Sarah's heart beating.

But it didn't really feel like a whole beat.

It only felt like half a heartbeat.

I felt the other half, in my own chest.

Our two hearts beat together—*ba-pum*, *ba-pum*, *ba-pum*—a deeper rhythm under the tapping of the raindrops on leaves and dirt and hat brims and horses.

We lay there, our hearts beating together, her blood on both of us.

I felt her heart, felt my Sarah's heart, beating between us.

And it didn't feel like it was dying.

It didn't feel like that at all.

I leaned back and looked into her eyes. There was trust in those eyes. And love. And there was a calmness there, too, and a steady strength.

"All right," I whispered to her.

I sat back on my heels.

"Out of the way now, son. You can look away if you want to."

"No," I said. "I was ready to say good-bye, sir, if I had to. But she ain't ready. She ain't ready yet. She's still got more living to do."

"Now, son, she's got a bullet in her neck and—"

"Is there a horse doctor in Yakima?" I interrupted.

"Well, yeah, of course. But Doc Stevens ain't gonna come all the way out here to see a horse that's just short of already dead."

"But if I took Sarah to him, he'd see her?"

"Sure he would, but, hell, boy, look at her. She won't make it to Yakima. She won't even make it to standing up."

"Yes. She will. If I ask her to."

I crouched down by her head, and we looked into each other's eyes again.

"You ready, girl?" I asked. She blinked.

I rubbed my hand up the bridge of her long nose and then grabbed hold of her bridle.

"Let's get up, Sarah. Come on."

She lifted her head off the ground. Then her neck. I rose with her, staying close, keeping my hands and my eyes on her. She brought her front legs up under her. Then she sat there, breathing hard.

"Good girl," I said. "That's my girl."

Then, with a grunt and a heave and probably with the help of an angel or two, my Sarah stood up with all four hooves in the mud.

She stood there, breathing hard and with her head down, but sure enough standing up.

"Well, I'll be," the man said behind me.

"Doc Stevens, you said his name was?" I asked. "In Yakima?"

"Yeah. Does people, mostly, but horses when he needs to."

"Thank you, sir. You are the posse, right, lawfully appointed?"

"Yes, we are. I am Sheriff McLeary, and I've deputized these men here in the pursuit of the wanted outlaw Caleb Fawney."

I pulled the sack of money out from my satchel and handed it up to him.

"Here's the money he stole from Mr. Campbell. This gray here is also Mr. Campbell's." I nodded toward the stallion. "I'd appreciate you seeing he gets back to him." Next I pulled Mr. Fawney's pistol out, and handed that up, too. "And this here's Mr. Fawney's gun." The sheriff took the sack and pistol without saying a word, his eyebrows raised. "You'll find Mr. Fawney up the trail a ways, 'bout two hundred yards up the draw. He's badly wounded, but not yet dead when I left him."

The sheriff whistled, low and surprised.

"He fall off his horse or something?"

"No, sir. I shot him."

The sheriff's mouth dropped open, but it seemed he was out of words. He just sat there looking at me.

"Now I best be getting this horse to the doctor," I said. I picked up Mr. Fawney's hat from where it lay in the mud and put it on my head, then walked away through the posse still up on their horses, leading my wounded Sarah behind me.

CHAPTER
22

When we got to Yakima, the doctor said that there was nothing he could do.

"I'm sorry," he said, pursing his lips and shaking his head.

"Sir," I replied, "I walked this horse five miles through the rain and the mud to get her to you. She's got strength in her. She'll live, if you treat her."

"There's a bullet in her neck! She can barely stand!" he protested. "I'm sorry, son, but there's just no way. I'd have to get that bullet out. And clean the wound. And stitch it up. Ain't no horse gonna put up with that. Ain't enough whiskey or morphine in the world to keep a horse calm enough to get through all that."

"I'll keep her calm for you, doctor. And I'll keep her standing. Please, sir."

"She'll have to be still. She'll have to be still through it all. Ain't no way she's gonna stand still if I'm digging a bullet out and putting in stitches."

"She'll stay still, sir. If I ask her to. She'll do it for me. Please."

Doc Stevens had been home, eating his lunch, when I'd come a-knocking. We were standing just outside his front door. Sarah was standing, head bowed, in his little front yard. She was a sure enough sorry-looking sight. One side of her was covered all in mud from where she'd been lying. The other was caked in dried blood from her bullet wound.

The doctor shook his head, looking at her. He looked back at me. He blew out his breath.

"Fine. I'll do what I can, if you can keep her standing, and standing still."

"Thank you, sir! Thank you!"

He held up a hand.

"Don't thank me, son. I'm telling you, she ain't gonna make it. She's lost a lot of blood, and she's about to lose even more. But we'll do what we can. Bring her on around to the stable in the back. I'll get my things."

The stable was dark and musty and smelled like it was seldom used. The doctor brought a flickering lantern in with him and hung it from a hook, casting a yellow light into the cramped space.

"All right," he said, zipping open a black leather bag and pulling out a variety of metal tools. "Let's get to it. I'll work just as long as she can stay still. When she gets to bucking and stomping, I'm putting her down. It'd be cruel not to."

I swallowed. My broken heart quivered at his words, but I kept my voice as strong as I could.

"Yes, sir. I understand."

I stood right in front of my Sarah, right square in front of her. I put both my hands on her cheeks and bent in close, locking my eyes on hers, big and brown. Her breathing calmed, and we both stood, each looking at the other.

"Stay with me, Sarah," I whispered right down into her heart. "Stay right here with me."

The doctor moved around over by her neck, over by that bleeding bullet hole. His hands came up, each holding metal.

He paused, and from the corners of my eyes I could see him look up at me.

"You ready, son?"

I closed my eyes and pressed my forehead up against Sarah's. I held her head tight in my hands. I touched my lips to the coarse fur of her nose. I said every prayer I've ever said or am ever gonna say, without saying a word. I felt for her heartbeat through my hands and found it and held it and added my own into it, so we were together.

"Yes, sir," I said. "We are ready."

And with a sigh and a breath, the doctor went to work.

Sarah tightened under my hands. Her muscles went all taut and her head started to pull back but I held it tight. I opened my eyes and looked right into hers and I held her tight, and strong, and steady.

"Easy," I whispered. "Easy, girl. Stay with me, Sarah."

Her eyes rolled and her nostrils flared and her breath came hot and fast but she stayed with me. She held steady with me. Her lips curled and her mouth opened but she stayed with me.

"That's it. That's it." I scratched at her jaw with my fingernails and kept my palms tight and warm against her.

"All right," the doctor said, stepping back and wiping at his forehead with his sleeve. "The bullet's out. Now I'll have to clean it. That'll sting something awful. Then it's stitches."

"Go, sir. We're ready."

He cracked his knuckles and reached for more tools and a little bottle.

"Here we go," he said.

Sarah stomped and her head reared back, but I caught her and held her. She let out a whinny, high and hurting, but I held her and she stayed still for me. I blinked away the tears that sprang to my eyes.

"It's all right, Sarah. It's all right." I squeezed my eyes shut and my head dropped down against hers and I let the tears seep through my lashes and down my cheeks. "It's all right, girl."

I could hear Doc Stevens working, could hear him bustling and breathing and licking his lips. He was hurrying as best he could, I could tell, and I was grateful.

"Almost there," he said. I let go my hard grip on Sarah's head. I rubbed my hands in slow, soft circles on her neck, her jaw, her cheeks. I whispered words to her, words of comfort and words of memory and words of promise. I blinked into her eyes and she blinked back into mine and we stayed together. We stayed together, Sarah and me, amidst all the world around us.

"Done," the doctor said, and a weepy, almost-crying kind of smile came to my face. I half laughed, half sobbed, and wiped my tears off on Sarah's nose. The doctor took a step back and mopped his brow. His arms hung slack at his sides and he looked at me, shaking his head.

"Son," he said, "I declare I have never seen anything like

that in all my days. A horse, standing still for stitches like that. And not bucking or kicking or nothing. Never seen anything like it."

"Well, you ain't never seen nothing like my Sarah," I said.

"I have," he answered. "I have seen plenty of horses in my day, all kinds. What I have never seen the likes of is you and that horse, together."

He sat back on a stool against the wall. Sweat was dripping down his neck and showing through on his shirt. I rested my cheek on Sarah's head and smiled.

"Now, son. We got the bullet out. And she's still standing. But that's about it. If I was a bettin' man, I wouldn't put my money on her making it through the night. I don't want your hopes up, is what I'm saying. Your horse is still more than likely gonna die."

"No," I said, calm. "She's not."

The doctor shrugged.

"Well. We'll see. Come on inside, son. I'll get you something to eat."

"No, thank you, sir. I'll stay with her, if that's all right."

He shrugged again.

"Suit yourself. There's oats in the bin there and the well's out back. If you can get anything in her, that'd be good. I'll check on you both this evening."

"Thank you, sir. Thank you so much."

"You're welcome." He patted Sarah on her back. "Good luck, horse."

*   *   *

I did not leave Sarah's stall the rest of that whole day. Or the night that followed, cold as it was. The good doctor brought me a blanket and some food and I slept right there on the stable floor, in a pile of straw, with my horse. I remembered Papa, never leaving Mama and Katie's side. And Ah-Kee never leaving Mrs. Davidson. Taking care is what we do, I s'pose. It's all we can do, really. All we can do is be there. And sometimes that's enough.

I kept waking all night long, jumping up with a start and feeling for Sarah in the darkness, reaching for her to make sure she was still standing, still with me. And she was, every time.

At some point I must have finally fallen into a sure enough deep sleep, because I awoke to the doctor creaking open the stable door and letting in the light of full-on morning. I jumped right up to my feet.

Sarah was there, still standing, but with her head low and her mouth open, breathing ragged.

"Well, I'll be," the doctor said, slapping Sarah lightly on the rump. "Look who's still here. Glad to see I was wrong about you again, horse." He looked over at me, rubbing my eyes and yawning the sleep out of my head. "There's someone here to see you."

The sheriff walked in and nodded at me. His tall frame filled up the shadowy stable.

"Morning, son," he said, holding out his hand. I shook it and nodded back.

"Good morning, sir." He cocked an eyebrow at Sarah and shook his head. "I see this horse of yours is still breathing," he said, with a half smile hiding under his bushy mustache. "She's making me look pretty foolish."

"No, sir." I grinned back. "But I s'pose she's making me look pretty smart."

He chuckled and held an envelope out to me.

I took it, then looked inside. I gasped. In the envelope was money. And plenty of it.

"What's this, sir?"

"That there is your reward, paid by the U.S. Marshal and the State of Washington. For the capture of one Caleb A. Fawney. Two hundred and fifty dollars, paid in full. Doc here is my witness."

I blinked and swallowed and looked up at him.

He frowned.

"I kinda thought you'd be pleased. That's a nice little sum of money."

"Yes, sir. It's just . . . well, how I got it, I s'pose. I never thought I'd kill a man, is all. And I certainly never thought I'd get paid for it."

"Huh. Well, if it eases your mind any, you didn't kill Caleb Fawney."

"He's alive?"

"Nope. Not remotely. But Mr. Caleb Fawney died by his

own hand, technically speaking. Shot himself as my posse rode up on him. Your shot didn't do him any good, but the fatal bullet came from his own gun."

"But I *took* his gun."

"Seems he had another. Little derringer. Reward's still yours, though, as the one most responsible for his death and capture. Congratulations, son."

I looked at the money, thinking. Fawney'd had another gun the whole time. He could've pulled it on me, could have shot me for spite or revenge or to try one last desperate escape. But instead he'd shared a drink with me, and wished me luck. And given me his hat.

I cleared a scratch from my throat.

"I owe Mr. Campbell," I said. "For my horse here."

The sheriff shook his head.

"John Campbell is already halfway to Walla Walla. Told me to thank you sincerely for getting him his money back, and that if anyone owes anyone anything, it's him owing you. The horse, he said, was already yours. He was pretty darn impressed with your grit, and he wishes you and your horse here the best."

"Thank you," I said quietly. I bent down and put the envelope into my satchel.

"So, where's your home, son?"

I looked down at the dirt stable floor. I didn't have no home. I didn't have no nothing, except for Sarah. I reached up and put my hands on her. She lowered her head and nuzzled my neck, soft and warm.

"She's right here," I answered. "Sarah here is my home."

The sheriff's eyebrows furrowed down.

"You ain't got somewhere to go?" he asked, his voice gruff. "Some family somewhere?"

I didn't answer. I didn't have the words for it. I kept my eyes and my hands on my horse.

"Well," the doctor said, "you're welcome to stay here as long as you need, Joseph."

"Thank you," I said, still looking at Sarah. "I appreciate that, sir."

"Will you come in for some breakfast, then?"

"No, sir. Thank you. I think I'll stay here with Sarah."

"I figured. I'll bring something out. And, Joseph . . . she ain't out of the woods. She's made it longer than I thought, but she's still not eating, and she's getting weaker all the time. You need to prepare yourself. She's put up a helluva fight— you both have—but the odds are still that she ain't gonna make it. You understand that?"

I nodded without looking up at him.

The sheriff shook my hand and wished me luck, and the two men left.

I stood there with Sarah. And she stood there with me. She rubbed her nose up against my shoulder. I scratched at her mane.

"Don't you go leaving me, girl," I whispered. "We're all that we've got, me and you."

*　　*　　*

Doc Stevens kept bringing me food, out there in the stable. Breakfast, and then lunch, and then a dinner. But it wasn't my eating I was worried about.

Then, finally, as the sun was setting and the night chill was coming on, Sarah did it. She shoved her nose in the feedbag I'd been offering her every hour and she started munching on those oats. My heart went right to thumping and I don't know if it was a half-beat or a whole but it was sure enough a *happy* beat.

I almost danced and sang right there, but I had to hold that feedbag for her.

"That's it!" I whisper-sang. "Eat up, girl! Eat up!" Sarah chewed her way right through that sack of oats and then, with big, slopping licks, she emptied the bucket of water I held up to her.

Tears were in my eyes, but for the first time in as long as I could remember they were happy tears.

I fed my Sarah on and off all night. Any time I woke up in that darkness I'd call her name and fumble for the bag and hold it out to her for as long as she ate.

When the doctor came in the morning I jumped right up.

"She's eating, Doc! She's been eating oats all night!"

The doctor raised his eyebrows.

"How much?"

I held up the feedbag.

"Three of these! And three buckets of water, too!"

The doctor looked at Sarah. She looked better, there

weren't no doubt about it. Her head was higher. Her ears perkier. Her eyes brighter. The doctor smiled.

"Well, I'll be," he said, shaking his head. "I'll be."

"So she's gonna be all right? She's gonna get better?"

Doc Stevens rubbed a thoughtful hand across Sarah's flank.

"I reckon she will, son." He shook his head again and laughed, just a little laugh. "I reckon she will. Now will you finally come on out of this barn and let this horse be alone for just a while?"

I wrapped my arms around Sarah's neck, a smile on my face to match the peace in my heart.

"I reckon I won't, Doc. I reckon I won't."

"Yep. I don't s'pose I would, either."

The doctor left, after taking a look under Sarah's bandages. He reckoned it'd be a couple more days before she'd be ready to do any traveling.

When he left, I sat down in my straw bed, back up against the stable wall. In a couple days, then, I'd be free to go. I'd have no horse to chase, no debt to pay, no man to find. No place to go.

I had my horse. And I had some money. And my papa's pistol. And a little black bird. And an outlaw's hat. But that was about it.

What I didn't have was a home.

But I s'pose, maybe, I had an idea.

The leaves were mostly gone off the trees, leaving the branches bare and alone against the fading light of the sky. Those leaves that were left were bright and beautiful, sure enough glowing in the colors of the sunset.

My sweet Sarah was strong and steady beneath me, my body moving with hers as we made our way up the empty road. Darkness fell around us like a blanket, but a cold one. Our breath puffed in white clouds that we left behind as we went. The river to our side had a fragile lace of ice at its edge.

I took the turn I knew to take, up off the main road. The light was almost gone, but I knew where I was going.

Then it was there, up ahead. The warm and welcoming light of a fire glowed in the cabin's window, and a trail of smoke rose from its stone chimney.

Around me and Sarah, a soft snow began to fall. Big, fluffy, silent white flakes, drifting and tumbling down. I looked up, watching them fall and flutter. Here and there, in the sky between the clouds, single stars were just beginning to spark and flicker.

I could feel a smile on my face, sure enough, but I was feeling a bit too much to say I was happy. I *was* happy, I s'pose, but I was lots of other things at the same time. I reckon I always will be.

Behind me, I could still hear the river talking. It was telling me a story, and I knew the voice that was doing the talking. There was plenty of sadness in the story, I reckon, but it wasn't sad all the way through. There was an awful lot of love, and an awful lot of together, and an awful lot of happy at the end. It was a good story, I thought. A good story.

Way up above me were campfires. Campfires of folks that had gone before me. They were together now, gathered, looking down at me. They were together. That was something. A beautiful kind of something. I looked up at them, and didn't bother about the blurriness in my eyes. I reckon they were smiling, too. I missed 'em, sure enough, true and deep and hard, but the loving was stronger than the missing.

And all around me were the feathers of angels, drifting down. Falling on my shoulders, and the brim of my hat. Angels that had been with me, no doubt, the whole way. I could hear Katie's voice, looking at those angel feathers. And I reckon I always will.

And in my pocket was a little bird, a little black stone bird. A memory I'd always carry. The memory of a friend.

And under me was a horse. A horse I shared my very heart with. Getting her back had been tough. But Papa had said that when there's something that's got to be done, the thing to do is just to buckle down and do it the best you can. And I had. Just like he'd have wanted me to. I'd gotten her back. My sweet Sarah. My sweet Sarah.

In the window was the shape of a person. A woman, it looked like, holding a baby. Just a silhouette, before a golden fire, in the darkness of a canyon night. The silhouette disappeared, and the cabin door opened.

Anna Davidson stood in the door, looking out at me.

"Joseph," she said.

"Mrs. Davidson," I answered. I patted Sarah on the neck and slid down off her back.

A boy came running past his mama, right out the door and through the falling snow. He hit me with a running hug that almost knocked me down and wrapped his arms tight around me.

"Joseph!" he hollered. "Joseph, you're back!"

I put my arms around him, too.

"Justin," I said, giving him a squeeze. "My Justin."

Mrs. Davidson took a few steps toward me, wrapping that baby up a little tighter in a blanket. Mr. Davidson stepped through the door behind her, then followed her out.

"Is this the horse, then?" she asked. "Is this your Sarah?"

"It is, ma'am. This is her."

"She's a fine horse," Mr. Davidson said.

"Yes," I said. "She sure enough is."

"It's good to see you, Joseph," Mrs. Davidson said, looking into my face. "Are you just passing through again?" she asked quietly, her eyes steady on mine.

I raised one hand from Justin's back and rested it up on Sarah, my sweet Sarah, standing by me. I looked up at the stars, through the falling snow, and listened to the river talking behind me. I reckoned, just maybe, you *can* choose your home.

"No, ma'am," I said, looking back at her. "I am not passing through. I'm coming home."

ACKNOWLEDGMENTS

I'm lucky to have a long list of folks I need to thank for all their support in making this book—and many other books, as well—come to life.

A huge thanks to my editor, Nick, as well as to Jeffrey, Jeremy, Sara, Bess, Charlie, Tracy, Nikki, Sue, Sheila Marie, Lizette, and the whole amazing crowd at Scholastic. I'm so happy and grateful to be with you. Also, Nina gets her own shout-out for another beautiful cover.

To my agent, Pam, and Bob Diforio, for all the help and support.

To my local community of writers, Write on the River, and to my writing group—it's so great to have so many great writers to share ideas and community with.

To the Fearless Fifteeners—one great year behind us, many more to come! Getting through a crazy, brain-spinning year was so much more fun with all of you!

To the wonderful staff and students of Mission View Elementary. One of the things I'm luckiest to have is a job that I wake up excited to go to, and that's because of all of you. Thanks for all the cheers and smiles.

To my friends, old and new, who have been nothing short of amazing in cheering me on and encouraging me. Thank you.

Lastly, but not remotely least, to my family. This book is, in many ways, mostly about family . . . and all of you were the inspiration for all the best parts. I can't thank you all enough.

ABOUT THE AUTHOR

Dan Gemeinhart is the author of several books for young readers, most recently *Scar Island*. His first novel, *The Honest Truth*, was a *New York Times* Editors' Choice selection, an Indie Next List selection, and an Amazon.com Best Book of the Month. His second novel, *Some Kind of Courage*, was an Amazon.com Best Book of the Year for 2016. A teacher-librarian and father of three daughters, he lives with his family in Washington State. Visit him at www.dangemeinhart.com.